Hitchhiker
Second Edition

by Donald Skiff

ISBN: 9781795532334

Table of Contents

Introduction to
the Second Edition

What is it like to be a person—a human being—living in this age? Until modern times, the question almost didn't have meaning, since everyone knew intuitively what a human was.

Well, maybe that isn't true; some of us have been considered sub-human because of the color of our skin or the degree to which we exhibited behavior we called "civilized."

Such ignorant views aside, most of us have what we think is a clear notion of what it is like to be a human. With the attention recently given to artificial intelligence, however, that clarity seems to be giving way to uncertainty.

"What is it like to be a bat?" is a question that caught my eye in recent writing about consciousness. It was expressed in:

> ... *a paper by American philosopher Thomas Nagel, first published in* The Philosophical Review *in October 1974, and later in Nagel's* Mortal Questions *(1979).*
>
> *In it, Nagel argues that materialist theories of mind omit the essential component of consciousness, namely that there is something that it is (or feels) like to be a particular, conscious thing.*

4

He argues that an organism has conscious mental states, "if and only if there is something that it is like to be that organism—something it is like for the organism to be itself.

We're not referring simply to differences in points of view, or even cultural or ethnic things, but "born-into" things such as the natural sensitivities to outside elements like the color of objects or the spectrum of sound waves that we hear. Bats, as we know, have a kind of radar by which they can perceive objects invisible to the human eye. Many species of whale use echolocation to find food and monitor other creatures around them, and they communicate with each other over thousands of miles of ocean.

And these are only creatures that we know about with our limited sensory apparatus. Many stories written over hundreds of years have speculated about hitherto undiscovered living beings that might at some time impact upon life as we know it.

The following stories are about such discoveries and what they might contribute to the question "What it is like to be a human?"

In this edition of the book, several stories have been added to The Hitchhiker, stories that extend the theme introduced in the first edition, for that theme inspired a number of questions beyond the original. It made more sense to expand the original book than to include them in a subsequent collection.

The first edition of this book included "The Troubadour," an entirely different story. In its place we have added the additional Hitchhiker stories.

Acknowledgments

I am indebted to Marjorie Lynn and Grace Stewart, whose literary critiques were invaluable for the First Edition of this book, and to the members of Writers Unlimited, a group dedicated to sharing our writing and our comments and suggestions.

And none of this would have been possible without the encouragement and suggestions of my wife, Judith.

The Hitchhiker

One

Walter usually drove the highway with cruise control engaged, but in the gathering dusk he disabled it because he needed to be more alert. There wasn't much traffic on the highway into the city, and he could see an occasional deer. He'd never hit one, although he'd had a couple of close calls. He had thought about getting one of those whistles for his front bumper that are supposed to scare them off, but hadn't gotten around to it.

He lived alone, by preference. Since his divorce six years before, he enjoyed his solitude. He expected to retire from the phone company in another year, and planned to do some traveling after that. In his spare time, he built furniture in his basement, relishing the smell of newly-cut wood and the rich odors of varnish and glue. Most of the finished pieces he gave away to friends.

A car was parked alongside the roadway, showing no lights. He slowed down and gave it extra space as he drove by. As he passed, he saw someone sitting behind the wheel. *Should have his lights on, or his blinkers,* he thought. Glancing in his rear view mirror, he wondered why he would be just sitting there at the side of the road. Maybe he had car trouble.

Pulling off the pavement and stopping, he backed up, watching the other car in his mirror. Within a car's length, he stopped. His backup lights showed a face, but he couldn't tell anything more. He sat there for a moment, wondering what to do—report the car to 9-1-1, and let the police handle it, or get out and at least offer his help. Could be dangerous, approaching a strange car at night on a deserted highway. He turned off the Rachmaninoff that had been playing on his radio.

Getting out and walking back to the parked car, he pulled his phone from his pocket. Because of the darkness, he couldn't see the person clearly, so he switched on the light on his phone.

She looked at him through the glass, terrified.

"Do you need help?" he asked, hoping she could hear him through the closed window. He couldn't blame her for not opening it if she was frightened, but when she didn't answer he repeated his question, louder. She still didn't respond.

He tapped on the glass. "I'm here to help, if you need it," he said, still louder.

She fumbled with the window control, and finally got it open. She still didn't say anything, just looked at him with fear covering her face.

"You should have your lights on, at least, ma'am," he said. "Do you need my help?"

Her voice was soft with apprehension. "I shouldn't be here," she said.

"If you're having car trouble, I can call somebody."
He leaned out and looked at her tires. Walking around
the car, he inspected the other tires.

"You don't have a flat. Will your car run?" Walter
glanced up and down the highway, feeling frustrated.
The woman was clearly confused and frightened.

"I shouldn't be here," she repeated.

"Can I give you a lift? I can take you into town if
you want."

It dawned on him that she was not functioning
very well. Her eyes darted around, at him, at his car,
at the dashboard of her car. *Maybe she's had a stroke*,
he thought. "I won't hurt you," he said, putting his
hand on the door handle.

She didn't seem to react to that, so he opened the
car door and extended his hand. "Looks like you might
have something wrong with you," he said quietly.
"Maybe you had a stroke. Let me take you in to the
hospital. Come on, I won't hurt you."

Hesitantly, she gave him her hand, and he led her
out of the car and around to the passenger side of his
own car. Helping her in, he said, "I'll get your purse
and lock your car, okay?"

Securing her car and returning, he got in slowly
to avoid frightening her more. In the dim interior
light, he smiled at her. "We'll get you some help," he
said gently. "Better buckle up."

When she didn't move, he reached across her and
fastened her seat belt. All the while, she simply stared
at his face, flinching slightly when he touched her, but
not making a sound.

Driving on, he thought of looking in her purse to get some identification or a number to call, but decided that it would be safer to wait and let the hospital people do that. He was pretty sure she'd had a stroke, or maybe a mental breakdown. Either way, he needed to hurry and not do anything to upset her more.

She continued to look at him without speaking. The fifteen-minute ride into town seemed longer. "If you had a stroke, you need medical help as soon as possible," he said.

"I shouldn't be here," she said again.

"Why? Doesn't anybody know where you are? Do you have family or somebody who can come and get you?"

She leaned over and kissed him on the cheek, startling him. She had a slight smile on her face. He glanced at her occasionally as he drove. *Looks like she can move all right. Wouldn't she be lopsided if she had a stroke? She doesn't seem afraid of me anymore.*

"She died," she said suddenly.

Walter looked at her. "What?"

"She died, and I guess it got us mixed up."

The hair stood up on the back of his neck. "Who?"

"I'm not supposed to be here."

He realized that he had been holding his breath. Letting it out suddenly, he slowed the car and looked at her. After a long moment, he said, "I think we have a problem."

She simply smiled at him.

There was nothing to do but continue. Walter felt something approaching panic, but he drove on, hoping that nothing bad would happen in the meantime. He hadn't thought of looking around in her car back there. Maybe she'd killed somebody, and they were stuffed in the back seat or the trunk. Maybe she had a knife in her purse. She hadn't paid any attention when he put it next to her. He glanced at her frequently.

Driving up to the emergency entrance of the hospital, he got out without looking at her and waved at the first person he saw inside. "I found this lady out on the highway. She's not injured that I can tell, but I think she may have had a stroke."

Attendants rushed out with a wheelchair and helped the woman into it. Walter followed after them. "She's confused," he said.

"We'll check her out. Are you her husband?"

"No, I just happened by and stopped. She was just sitting in her car at the side of the road, and she hasn't said two words."

"Could she walk?" One of the attendants took a clipboard from a desk.

"Yes," Walter said. "She doesn't seem lopsided— isn't that a sign of a stroke?"

"Could be. But we'll check. You don't know her, you say?"

"No."

"Would you fill out this form?" The attendant with the clipboard handed it to Walter, while the other one wheeled the woman into triage.

"She has a purse—I'll get it," said Walter, turning toward the door.

When he returned, the woman was lying on a gurney, and people were trying to talk to her. She kept looking at Walter, fear showing on her face. A female doctor looked up at him. "She seems to know you," she said. "Maybe you can get her to speak to us?"

Walter felt committed. He approached the woman and took her hand. "Can you tell the doctors what's wrong?" he asked, feeling inadequate.

By that time she was connected to various machines, and kept looking around at the doctors and nurses, apprehension showing on her face.

"These people are here to help you," Walter said.

"Can you tell us your name?" someone asked.

Walter handed them the woman's purse, which he had been holding. A nurse opened it and withdrew a wallet. "Abigail DeVoe," she said. "Nineteen sixty-four. Lives in Braille."

"A phone?" someone asked.

"No." the nurse continued to rummage through the purse. "No phone numbers, either."

A doctor shook his head. "Why don't people carry identification!"

"Any medical ID?"

"No. One credit card."

"She's had an MI," said a doctor who had been monitoring the woman with a stethoscope. "Sounds okay now, though."

"Get her to the cath lab, stat," ordered another.

"Stay here, please," said a nurse to Walter. He found a nearby chair and sat down.

In a moment, another nurse came to him. "So you don't know this woman?"

"No. I just found her on the highway. She seemed confused. I thought this would be the best place to bring her."

"Good thinking. But we need to find out who she is. Would you object to talking with a policeman?"

Walter sighed. "No," he said, but felt impatient.

In a few minutes, a doctor came out from the treatment area. "She's okay, physically. She's had a serious myocardial infarction—a heart attack—recently, but not a stroke. Maybe a TIA. She'll need to see her regular physician as soon as possible." He smiled. "She's not very talkative."

Walter frowned. "So what are you going to do with her?"

The doctor shrugged. "Let her go. Maybe you can help her get home."

Walter sighed. "Why me?"

The nurse smiled at him. "You're the good Samaritan," she said. "Otherwise, it's the police."

She helped the woman into a wheelchair to take her out to the car. At the curb, the nurse stepped close to Walter and spoke in a low voice, "That resident asshole just wanted to get rid of her. I think she may have had a TGA—Transient Global Amnesia—a kind of amnesia that will clear up in a few hours. It's not usually serious, but she should see her own doctor as soon as possible."

A few minutes later, the two of them sat in his car, still at the entrance to the emergency room. Walter sighed. "Abigail—that's your name?" When she didn't respond, he said, "Your driver's license says you live in Braille. I'll drive you there. Maybe you can connect with your folks. You do have folks there, right?"

Braille was sixty miles away. At the outskirts, Walter pulled into a highway rest area. "I have to use the restroom," he said to the woman, who smiled back at him. "You want to go in, too, or wait out here?"

"I shouldn't—" she began, and he finished it for her: "be here. I know. Okay, just wait here. Don't leave the car."

He hurried into the rest room, suddenly aware that he had been holding his urine for some time.

Back at his car, Abigail sat motionless, other than watching him walk out of the shelter.

"Okay," he said, "I need your address." He reached tentatively for her purse, expecting her to clutch it to her, as most women would. But she still didn't move, simply watching his face with that faint smile on hers.

He pulled her billfold out of the purse, deliberately keeping it and his hands up where she could see them. "One-one-two-one Richmond Street," he read aloud from her driver's license. Turning to the GPS instrument on his dashboard, he entered the address and waited for the confirmation and directions. The female voice visibly startled Abigail. She stared at the instrument.

Walter started the car and pulled out onto the highway. "Now at least we know where we are going," he said. The path to the address was simple, and a few minutes later they pulled up before a large condominium-type building.

"I may need your keys," he said, "in case there's no one else there." He pulled a small key ring from her purse. Besides a key to her car, there were just two other keys. One of them, he decided, must be to her apartment. "Okay, let's go see who you are."

He led her up the stairs to the door to her apartment. He knocked loudly. There was no sound coming from inside. He knocked again; still no response.

"Okay," he said to Abigail, who had meekly followed his lead all the way to the door without any indication that she knew where they were. "We're going in, okay?"

He put the key in the lock and opened the door. "Hello!" he called before entering. The apartment seemed unoccupied. He and Abigail stood just inside the door, looking around at an ordinary apartment. Leading her to a sofa, he gestured to her to sit down, and then explored the rest of the apartment.

As he went, he kept talking to her. "The nurse said you might have had an attack of amnesia, not a stroke. She said it should clear up in an hour or so."

A couple of framed photos stood on top of a spinet-style piano, one showing Abigail alongside a young man, the other showing an elderly couple, evidently taken some decades earlier. On the refrigerator, a note said simply "8:00"

Walter glanced at Abigail, who sat seemingly unaware of where she was. She looked at him occasionally, and smiled. *Doesn't look like she's going to give me any trouble,* he thought, *but she's no help, either.*

"This is obviously where you live," he said to her. "Do you live alone?" To answer his own question, he opened the refrigerator. "Just the food of a woman who lives alone," he said. "A half-eaten casserole of some kind, milk, Coke, tonic water." That prompted him to open the freezer door. Sure enough, a bottle of good gin, along with some store-bought frozen food.

Extracting the gin and a bottle of tonic water, he took two glasses from a kitchen cabinet. "Well," he said to her, "I need to think." He dispensed ice from the refrigerator door and mixed two drinks. Sitting beside Abigail, he put one drink in front of her and sipped from the other. "You owe me this much," he mumbled, gesturing with his glass.

Looking around the room, he noticed an old wall-mounted phone, and a desk that might reveal something he could use to identify this woman. *The phone won't help, unless the phone number happens to be printed on the dial, the way they used to do. The desk will be the place to start.*

"You're very kind," Abigail said suddenly.

Walter looked at her quickly. "Well, you can speak!"

"You're very kind," she repeated.

"Do you want a drink?" he asked, pointing at her glass and taking another large sip from his. "I sure need one right now."

She looked at the glass sitting before her, but didn't answer. Then she looked at him and smiled.

Abigail was a little younger than Walter. Reasonably attractive, well-groomed graying hair and decent clothing. A skirt, sensible shoes. Her eyes on his pulled at him, but he kept his distance. It had been a long time since he'd felt that about a woman.

"Can you tell me anything about yourself?" he asked. "You said you shouldn't be here—wherever 'here' is. And you said, 'she died.' What does all that mean?"

"I shouldn't be here," she said, pointing to herself. "She died, and I'm here now. I don't know what to do." Her face looked worried.

Walter frowned, then gave a quick laugh, but caught himself. "You mean, you are not Abigail? You're only in her body?" When she nodded, he slumped, his mouth dropping open, and stared at her.

"That's why you don't know this place!" He drained his glass. A picture began to form in his mind. He had found her sitting quietly in a car parked at the side of the highway, and the doctors in the E.R. said she had suffered a heart attack. "Abigail what's-her-name had a heart attack on the highway and died," he said. "Then who are you? *What* are you?"

She simply smiled at him.

He reached over and grasped her arm lightly. "Are you some kind of spirit or something?" By this time, he was sweating. "Now, don't tell me you're some kind of zombie. I don't believe in those things. Those are just in the movies."

"I'm here to observe." She spoke as casually as a woman who had just walked into his office. "There was a mistake. I shouldn't be here." She again pointed to her chest.

Walter was speechless for a long moment. "You're kiddin' me, right? You're pretending to be some alien from outer space. Who put you up to this? Charlie and Shep? Those guys have a weird sense of humor, they could do it—but who are *you?*"

"I don't understand much of your language," she said. "I am trying."

He got up and made himself another drink. Standing before her, he managed to say, "You're inside her, but you don't know anything about Abigail?"

"She seems to have some kind of memory, not just before she died, long ago memory. I don't know this place." She gestured around the room. "This was her place?"

He sat down again, at a distance from her. "I guess so. It was on her driver's license." Turning toward her, he asked, "Were you in her when she died? Did you kill her?"

"No. Her life stopped, and I was transferred in. They made a mistake."

"Who made a mistake?" The glass in his hand was shaking, so he put it down on the coffee table.

She shrugged her shoulders.

"Did they kill Abigail?" Walter was having difficulty breathing. "Are they going to kill me?"

"No. They don't do that."

"Well," he breathed out, "I'm sure glad of that. I think."

Neither spoke for several minutes. Walter finished his second gin and tonic. Then he stood up again and faced her. "I don't know what I'm supposed to do! My mind is gone!"

"You are very kind," she said.

He felt that she meant it. Somehow, there was a real person in there, in that dead woman's body. She wasn't some robot or a zombie. She sounded like a real woman. Only she didn't know anything, either. She didn't know what to do. Some alien computer someplace had hit a snag and put her in the wrong body.

"When I first came up to you," he said, "out there on the highway, you looked scared to death. Were you?"

"Yes," she said simply. And then she said, "I was afraid you were going to kill me."

"Why?"

"It's my first assignment. Is that the word? Others said some of you are dangerous."

He scratched his head. "Wait. Wait. You are not Abigail. You're just inhabiting her body. What were you before that?"

She suddenly smiled broadly. "Abigail doesn't have a word for that."

"Oh, shit." He flopped back down on the sofa.

After a few moments of silence, he looked at her. "Then you don't know why she was out there on the highway." He pointed to the refrigerator. "There's a note on the fridge that just says, 'eight o'clock.' I guess that's what it means. You don't know anything about that, either?"

"No."

Another silence.

"She feels something," she said. "I don't know what that is."

"Oboy. That makes two of us." He thought for a while. "Well, here's an idea. Maybe she's hungry. We could do something about that. Or—" and he tried to come up with the words. "If she's now a live human being, or at least part of one, do you know if she needs to use the bathroom?" His face turned scarlet.

"I don't know. She feels something," and she pointed to her abdomen, "here."

"Oh, Christ!" He turned his face away for a moment, then, "Well, if she's hungry, that's easy. Let's try that one."

He took a couple of meals from the freezer, unwrapped them, and put them into the microwave. Then he went back to her. "I'm a terrible nurse," he said. "Sooner or later you're going to need more help than I can give you. I hope eating will do it for now."

"They didn't prepare me for this." She smiled at him.

"Nobody prepared me for this, either!"

When the microwave signaled, Walter retrieved the two meals, set them onto plates and took tableware from a drawer. Sitting beside her on the sofa, he put a plate of food before her. "I hope you know what to do with this." He demonstrated by eating from his own plate.

She copied his motion, put a forkful of food in her mouth, and smiled at him.

"Swallow," he said, again demonstrating.

She mirrored his motion, then put her fork down and lowered her head, smiling. "I'm teasing you," she said quietly.

"Oh, shit!" He flopped back on the sofa. "Now you're making fun of me. *I don't know what to do with you!*"

Still smiling, she said, "Some things are easy. As soon as the food touched my mouth, I knew what to do with it, just from how her body responds." She reached over and touched his hand. "Like this."

He grinned in spite of his tension. "You know, I think Abigail must have been a pretty nice person. You remind me of a robot—do you know 'robot'?"

She thought for a moment, then nodded. "You remind me of a robot I saw a few months ago. It was a demonstration of programming, and they showed us how every little movement, every gesture, had to be planned and programmed into that robot. But you seem to be able to speak, and move, and even feel, when you didn't know anything about Abigail three hours ago."

"There are parts of her brain that know a lot of things. Only—what happened just before she died— those don't work anymore. She still has some memory, and knowledge about how her body works, and some feelings—" She pointed to her abdomen, "I don't know what that means."

They ate silently. Walter glanced frequently at Abigail, wondering what was going on in her mind and what was going on in the mind of the *whatever it was* that was animating her.

She looked directly at him. "She was called Abigail. Are you called something?"

"Walter."

"You are Walter." After a long silence, "I wish—I wish I were Abigail."

"I guess you are, in a way. You look like her—" He got up and retrieved one of the photos from the piano. Thrusting it before her, he said, "You look just like this."

"Oh, my goodness!"

"But you don't know who this man is next to her?"

"No."

Walter put the photograph back. "I'm guessing that that young man is in for a shock."

She continued to eat the food.

"Your gin and tonic is pretty diluted by now," he said, picking up the glass.

"Is it nutritious?"

He grinned. "Only psychologically."

"You became—looser. Less tense."

He laughed out loud. "I guess I did. I was wound up pretty tight."

"Did it help you think?"

"You know," he said, "you're pretty perceptive. Is that Abigail?"

Smiling, she shook her head slowly. "Maybe."

"Let's try another one, okay?" He went to the refrigerator and mixed another gin and tonic. Handing it to her, he cautioned, "It's pretty strong. It will feel warm in your throat."

Abigail drank the whole thing without pausing.

"Wow," he said, grinning, "how does that feel?"

"As you said, 'warm.' I didn't know what to expect, but it felt familiar."

"She had the bottle in the freezer. People do that when they like to drink it straight."

"Straight?" Then after a thought, she said, "without the water, right?"

"Most people just take little sips." He demonstrated, and she laughed.

Walter sat down next to her. "You know, we still don't know what we're going to do. I don't have a clue, but I don't think I can leave you alone right now."

"You're very kind—Walter."

"Why are you here—there?" He pointed to her forehead. "You just said to observe. What's that mean?"

"I am to spend a time like this—only not here." She pointed to herself.

"How much time?"

She frowned. "I will be in a number of bodies before returning."

Walter took a deep breath and let it out. Then he flopped back against the sofa. Shaking his head, he said, "I don't understand."

"I need to know about you. Not just Walter. All Walters."

"An anthropologist?"

"I don't know that word."

"They do what you're here for, except they don't take over someone's body."

"Humans do that, too?"

"Yes. But—who were you supposed to occupy? You said you shouldn't be there, in Abigail's body. Whose, then?"

"Not a female. Someone who had just died, nearby."

He ran his fingers through his hair. "Have to be someone who just died without great damage to the body."

"Yes."

"Like Abigail, only somebody else."

"Yes."

"I need another drink, but I better not. I have to figure out what we're going to do." He looked steadily at her. "You are a whole lot smarter than I am. What are we supposed to do?"

"They are working on it."

"What? Who?" He sat up suddenly. "How do you know?"

"They've told me."

"Oh, shit!" He collapsed again against the sofa back. "What'd they say?"

"They don't use words, as you do."

"So we just wait?"

She smiled. Abigail smiled. "In our training, we learn how to slow our perceptions down to fit your sense of time."

Walter closed his eyes.

Then the telephone rang.

He hesitated until the phone rang four times. "Hello?"

A man's voice asked, "May I speak with Abigail?"

Walter took a deep breath. "Uh, she can't come to the phone right now. Do you know Abigail?"

The voice hesitated. "Yes. She and I were supposed to meet this evening."

Walter sighed again. "What's your name?"

"Michael. Abigail and I were supposed to meet at eight o'clock, and she hasn't shown up yet. Is she there?" His voice sounded young, and worried. "Is she all right?"

"Uh, do you know where she lives?"

"Yes."

"I think it might be good if you came here."

"What's wrong? Who are you?"

"Please come." Walter waited for a moment, then hung up the receiver.

Abigail was watching him closely as he returned to the sofa.

"I feel like I'm responsible for you," he said, "but I don't know what to do. If this guy knows Abigail, maybe he can at least help me here. *I don't know what to do!*"

Abigail pushed the coffee table away from the sofa. Then she moved over to Walter, lifted her skirt and straddled him. "I know what the feeling is now," she said softly.

His mind spiraled out of control. With practiced hands, Abigail unbuckled his belt and exposed him. Then she readied her own clothing and melted into him and him into her.

Sometime later, they lay entwined and smiled at each other dreamily.

"Was that Abigail?" he asked.

"Only the physical."

"Oh. Oh. That's putting it direct," he said. "Are you—I'm feeling really weird." He pointed at her forehead. "Are you male or female?"

"We don't have that distinction," she said.

"Oh boy." He looked at the ceiling. "I just had sex with an asexual being performing in a dead woman's body."

Abigail smiled. "It was an interesting experience," said the being.

They stood and straightened their clothing. Walter went into the bathroom, feeling almost dizzy. His reflection in the mirror grinned at him.

When he returned, Abigail was seated on the sofa, her hand exploring under her skirt. Walter laughed. "That's like in the movie," he said. "Under the Skin."

She looked at him, perplexed.

"It's about an alien," he said, then stopped. "Oops."

"What's a movie?"

He sat beside her. "I've had a lot to drink," he said with a little laugh. "A movie is a play that is recorded and played back for an audience." He looked at her and laughed again. "I'm not making any sense at all, am I?"

"I'm here to observe," she said matter-of-factly.

"People make up stories about themselves, about others, about events. Someone made up a story about a being from outer space—maybe like you—who puts on a disguise so people think she's human, and then she lures people—men—into a place where their bodies are dissolved into some kind of nutrient for her compatriots. She is catching food for her kind. Does that make sense?"

Abigail made a face. "We don't need that kind of nutrient."

"No, I didn't mean—"

"Are you afraid of me?"

"I'm going to have that other drink," he said, and got up to head for the kitchen.

"Would you make me one, too?"

He turned and looked at this woman with whom he had just made love. *How is it possible?* he thought. *She's playing with me. She's a setup. Charlie and Shep have set me up.* He laughed, and continued to the refrigerator. *Those crazy bastards!*

When he returned, Abigail smiled at him as she took the drink from him and sipped it.

"C'mon," he said. "You're not really an alien, are you? Did Charlie and Shep put you up to this? You've done a really good job, by the way." He drank his gin and tonic to the bottom of the glass.

She looked at him and smiled. "I am trying to understand your words."

"Forget it." Walter wanted to go back and chug directly from the gin bottle until it was empty.

"We coupled," she said seriously. "It was interesting. Do all humans do that?"

"A lot," he said. "Male and female."

She was delighted. "My goodness!" Pulling her skirt up, she looked down at herself. Then she looked up at him. "Show me."

"You are unbelievable."

"I'm here to observe," she said.

Walter hesitantly dropped his pants to show Abigail—no, the 'being'—what a male human looks like. She—or it—wasn't disappointed.

He quickly put his clothing back together. "You don't have this, where you come from?" he asked.

"No. What's the purpose of this?"

He felt as though she were taking notes. "It's how we procreate," he said.

"The sensations," she said, "were very complex. Does it have to do with why I kissed you, in the car after you had rescued me?"

"Maybe."

"I felt something then—Abigail felt something—that was similar. You were very kind, Walter. She felt drawn to you."

"I guess it's called 'bonding'. What I felt a little while ago, when we made love."

"Love?"

"It's that feeling, when one person is drawn to another—usually of the opposite sex."

"When I said I wish I were Abigail."

"Maybe."

"So interesting."

"How do you procreate?"

"Multiply?"

"Yes."

"We don't."

He looked at her in a new way. "Really?"

"We all come from a single 'song'."

"Song?"

"It's the only word that seems close. The beginning of music."

"You have music?" Walter cocked his head and smiled. Then he picked up her half-finished glass of liquor and drained it. She watched him, amused. "That's the only way I know how to describe it," she said. "You have music—they told us you do." "Yes." "Songs—our version of your songs—spring from individuals, and grow into new individuals." "Wow." *Like memes,* he thought.

"So," she said, looking at him as she had when she said she wished that she were Abigail, "perhaps that is how we procreate."

"That's beautiful!"

She shrugged. "We haven't had enough songs lately," she said. "That's why I'm here. That's why we are here—to search for songs."

He shook his head. "I don't believe it." Still, he did. Looking at this woman, this very human woman, whose arms around him he had felt just minutes ago, Walter realized that he had been missing something very important in his life, something he glimpsed at this moment. "I wish I could give you a song," he said.

Suddenly overcome, he retreated to the bathroom once more. Without glancing in the mirror, he sat on the commode for a long time.

When he returned, Abigail had gone into the bedroom and was lying on the bed, very still. He lay down next to her. "Are you all right?"

"They have repaired the error," she said softly. "Good bye, Walter."

And that was the end of it, of everything. Of Abigail. Of something that Walter couldn't describe, surely would tell no one, but would never forget. He went into the living room and sat motionless on the sofa.

Sometime later, he opened the door of Abigail's apartment to a stranger, the young man of the photo on the piano. "She's in there," Walter said, pointing. "She died in her sleep."
Walter stayed behind while the young man went into the bedroom and cried over Abigail's lifeless body.

After writing him a note about the location of her car on the highway, Walter let himself out quietly.

Two

Walter, Charlie and Shep sat in a corner booth of The Daily, an off-the-boulevard bar near their office in the telephone company. It was Friday afternoon.

"McKenzie told me today that they're cutting back again the first of the month," Shep said, looking closely at his shot glass that was nearly empty.

"They're always planning to cut back," Walter said.

"We got nothing to worry about," Charlie said, swiveling around to watch the sharp-looking woman who had just entered. "They need us."

The three of them had been friends for seventeen years, when they were all transferred into their department on the same day. Their Friday drink before heading home was a tradition since Walter's divorce, six years ago. They didn't talk about anything important; since none of them were sports fans, their conversations usually centered around work and women. Charlie and Shep were married, and sometimes they envied Walter, whose wife had left him for an airline pilot. Walter had been cynical about women ever since, and the other two men used his experience to justify their own lukewarm dedication to their wives. Friday night was their night.

They'd each had a couple of straight shots. Charlie, in particular, watched the other patrons of the bar as they talked. Walter attended to his drink.

"Y'know," Walter said, "we look around here—and at work, too—at the people and we think everybody is just like us."

"What d'ya mean?" asked Shep.

"Just regular people." Walter finished his drink. "And we never think that, like that guy in the yellow jersey over there, he could be *observing us.*

"So what?" Charlie half stood up, addressing the guy in the jersey. "Hey, here I am, what do you make of this?"

Jersey simply looked away.

Shep laughed. "You're crazy, Charlie. Sit down. You trying to start a fight?"

"No," said Walter, "I mean there are *observers*—just watching us."

Shep looked at Walter seriously. "You mean like the NSA?"

"Who cares about the NSA? No, I don't know, I just—I just think sometimes that there are people—

or what we think are people—out there, just *observing us.*"

"Whoa," said Shep. "Like aliens from outer space, like in the movies?" He had a disbelieving grin on his face.

Charlie looked at Walter. "Hey, Buddy," he said, "you going ape on us here?"

Walter lifted his empty glass to his lips, as though to distract himself from the subject. Then he got up, picked up his glass and asked, "Anybody else ready for another one?"

Charlie pushed the other two glasses toward him without saying anything. When Walter left the table toward the bar, Charlie looked at Shep. "That's not like him."

"I think our friend needs some soft company," said Shep.

"He's never said anything like that before." Charlie turned to watch Walter across the room. "He was always the one to poo-poo that stuff about alien invasions—or even the idea of other life in the universe."

"Is it paranoia?" asked Shep.

"Sounds like it." Charlie smiled up at Walter, who had returned with their drinks.

"I know you're talking about me," Walter said.

"We're just wondering, Pal," Shep said, smiling.

"I know, it sounds crazy. But—" Walter slid into the booth. The other two waited for him to explain.

"I had an experience last week." Walter described his finding a confused woman in her car on the highway, taking her to the E.R. where they said she'd had a heart attack, and taking her to her home in Braille, where she revealed "her" true nature. He didn't mention having sex with her or that she died.

"You think she was just shitting you?" asked Charlie.

Walter grinned. "For a while I was convinced that you two had put her up to it, to string me along."

"How would we know you'd stop on the highway for a stranded motorist?"

"We didn't even know you'd be there at that time," added Shep.

"Yeah, that's what I finally decided." He looked up at the others. "Not that you guys wouldn't ever do anything like that."

They all laughed.

"Then what do you think was going on?" asked Shep.

"She might have been schizoid," said Charlie. "You're lucky she didn't pull a knife on you."

"By the end," Walter said, "she had me pretty convinced. I wanted to get out of there, but if she really had had a heart attack, I couldn't just leave. Then some guy called on her phone, and he evidently knew her, so I asked him to come over. And I left."

"Weird," said Shep.

Charlie looked across the room. "That why you picked out that guy in the yellow jersey? You think he was really watching us?"

"No," said Walter. "Oh, I don't know."

"You're paranoid," said Shep. "She's got you paranoid. I would be, too. That was weird."

33

"What'd she act like?" asked Charlie, "you just said she acted confused. But when she said she was an alien, she get that bug-eyed look?"

Shep made a face to illustrate the look, and all three laughed.

"No, she acted just like an ordinary woman, but she didn't seem to know a lot of stuff everybody knows."

"Like what?"

"Well, there was a bottle of gin in her freezer."

The others laughed.

"I made up a couple of gin and tonics, cause if she had the stuff she must drink it, you know? But I had to show her how to do it." Walter frowned.

"Whoa," said Shep.

"And how to eat a pot pie that she had in her own freezer."

"You sure it was her place?"

"That's what her driver's license said. And it was her pictures in the apartment."

"Okay," said Charlie, "you have my permission to be paranoid." He looked around. "The guy in the jersey is gone."

All three silently scanned the crowded room.

That evening, Walter sat listening to a Sibelius recording, and thought about Abigail. Then he reminded himself that Abigail was dead. He wondered about the young man who had come to her apartment. Son? Lover? Would he talk if Walter tried to get in touch with him? But she was dead when the guy arrived. How would he even know about the alien? No, he decided, better close that door.

But maybe the guy thought that I had something to do with Abigail's death. Maybe right now he's trying to find out who I am. I'd sure be suspicious if I was him.

The next day Walter went to his favorite store, *Lumber and Cabinetry* just to browse through the aisles and inhale the wood smells. There was nothing in particular he needed for his projects, so he flipped through some magazines in the magazine rack.

"Fun, isn't it?" came from beside him.

He turned to see a small woman in work clothes. She was older, he guessed at least sixty, with short straight hair that was going from gray to white at her temples. Her hands were those of a craftsman. (*Craftsperson*, he corrected his unspoken thought.) "I like to just look at how they design things," he said.

"You build?" she asked.

"Yes."

"So do I, when I can get the time," she said. Her voice was husky, almost like a man's.

"What do you like to make?" Walter asked.

"Lots of things. I just like to work with my hands." Her smile seemed vaguely conspiratorial.

He looked around the store. "There's plenty in here to tempt you, isn't there?"

"There is."

Walter put the magazine he'd been holding back in the rack, and turned toward the door. "Good hunting," he said to the woman. He didn't wait for her to respond.

Driving home, he thought about women. *There's all kinds, some good, some like Daniele. That little gray-haired woman I bet you could trust.*

Daniele had been his wife, until she left after twelve years of marriage. She had blindsided him, coming home from a trip to announce that she was leaving him. She'd always been impulsive—charming when she was young, annoying as the years went on. Taking refuge in his basement cabinet shop, he'd questioned whether he should ever have gotten married in the first place.

Back home fixing himself a sandwich for lunch, he thought of the gray-haired woman, wondering what her woodworking projects were like. And then he thought again about Abigail. He realized that he felt a touch of grief for her, especially when he remembered the sex. *That's sick,* he thought. *She wasn't really a woman. What was she? She sure acted like a woman.*

Then he got a phone call from the Braille police. They wanted to talk with him about Abigail. They'd tracked him down from the information he'd given at the E.R.

He offered to go to Braille to talk to them, preferring not to have the police show up at his home or his office. When he got there he told them about finding Abigail and taking her first to the emergency room and then to her apartment, thinking that she would recover from the apparent heart attack.

"I know, it was wrong to just leave," he said, "but I didn't know the young fellow who showed up, and I didn't know what to tell him. I thought I could just disappear."

The officer, attractive in a prim sort of way, smiled wryly. "It looked suspicious, it sure did. But the people at the E.R. said you seemed on the up and up." She looked through her file. "Since the woman had suffered a heart attack in her car, apparently, and then died from another one in her home, there wasn't much to indicate foul play."

The following week, Walter, Charlie and Shep were kept busy, and didn't get together for lunch or Friday drinks. Nothing more was said about Walter's "paranoia."

On Saturday, he made an excuse to go to the wood store. Sure enough, the little gray-haired woman was there, buying plywood. "What's that going to be?" he asked her.

"An old-fashioned dish cupboard."

"With glass doors?"

"Oh, no. Ordinary folks back then didn't have glass except in windows. This'll be painted, with stenciled flowers on the doors. What do you make?"

"I'm working on a desk chair," he said. "Cherry."

"I'd love to see it." There was an impish quality to her, with that conspiratorial smile.

As he watched her selecting a four-by-eight piece of three-quarter inch plywood from the rack, he marveled at her strength, especially since her arms barely spanned the board. "You been at this a long time," he said.

She turned and grinned at him. "All my life. My father taught me cabinet making."

"You inherit his tools, too?"

"You bet." She placed the selected plywood on her cart. You want to see my shop?"

"Yeah. When's a good time?"

"Right now. Lemme check out and you can follow me. It's only six blocks."

Walter felt a giddiness that had not revealed itself in years. Here was somebody who felt the way he did about building things, somebody he might be able to share his interest with. That it was a woman added something he couldn't quite identify. Certainly, she wasn't the kind of woman he'd always known, and there wasn't any sexual energy between them.

Driving behind her pickup truck, he realized that the little feeling he had toward this woman was · *safety*. It made him smile.

She lived in a small old house that had a barn instead of a garage—something that had been built a hundred years ago when the neighborhood was at the edge of town, He pulled into the unpaved driveway behind her truck, stopped and went up to the back of her pickup. Lifting the plywood out, he carried it toward the barn, where she was opening the door.

"Thank you," she said, and led him to a large table sitting in the middle of the room. "Right there would be perfect."

The machinery in the barn was all ancient. She'd said that her father had taught her cabinet making, and this had evidently been his shop. Walter identified a large wood-turning lathe, a table saw, a planer and a joiner, and a drill press with a mortiser mounted on it.

"I'm impressed," Walter said.

She wiped her hands on a rag and picked up a small end table, not yet finished. "You said you worked in cherry," she said, holding it out to show him. "Solid cherry."

"Beautiful."

"Old cherry naturally darkens with age, but folks don't want to wait that long these days, so I'm staining it. It's for a friend of mine."

"It tickles me to run into somebody who loves wood as much as I do," Walter said.

She grinned.

"You do this for a living?" Walter asked.

"In a manner of speaking," she answered with a chuckle. "I work with contractors who are building homes."

"I don't know your name," he said.

"Jezebel. Call me Jez."

"I'm Walter. I work for the phone company, but my real work—" He gestured toward the machines, "I don't get paid for." He took out his phone and pulled up some photographs of his cabinet work.

"You give all those away?"

He shrugged. "I just enjoy making them."

"Awesome."

Walter moved toward the door. "Don't want to keep you from your work," he said, "thanks for showing me your shop."

Jez pulled a business card from her pocket. "Gimme a call when you want to chat about wood."

He extracted one of his own cards from his wallet. "Yeah. Same here."

∽——∾

One evening several weeks later, Jez phoned him. "Just wondering if you'd care to have a cup of coffee with me," she said.

He agreed, and put the lid back on a can of wood stain that he'd been stirring. He'd thought of the woman often since they had talked in her wood shop, but Walter had never been very gregarious. He hadn't learned the joys of small talk.

In the Denny's downtown, Jez waved at him rather awkwardly from a booth. Neither of them offered a hand to shake, but simply smiled at each other when he sat down.

"Get your cherry chair finished?" she asked, and laughed at the words. "Cherry-chair."

"Still sanding. My projects take a lot of time. I was just stirring some stain when you called."

"I figured you were the meticulous type."

A waiter interrupted them, and left promptly with their order for coffee.

Jez looked at Walter and pulled her hair behind an ear. "I have a friend," she began, choosing her words carefully, "who asked me to look you up."

40

Walter looked at her quickly. She wasn't smiling. "Should I be flattered or worried?" he asked, frowning.

"Probably flattered." She paused, looking directly at him.

After a long moment, she continued, "You met this friend about a month ago."

Walter's curiosity was up, trying to think of someone he might have met. The first one he thought of was Abigail, but he immediately discarded that thought. *She's dead.*

Jez, her face still serious, seemed to be struggling to find her words. "This friend seems to think that you are an open kind of person."

Walter shook his head. "You got me. I don't remember—"

"Yes you do," she said. "You met them out on Route Fifteen, just about dark."

She was watching him carefully.

Walter felt sweat run down his face next to his eye, making him blink.

"See, you do remember."

"Abigail?"

"Bingo. Only Abigail's dead."

Walter shook his head slowly. Chills went down the backs of his arms. "I don't understand."

"Yes you do."

He felt a surge of denial in his throat. "Are you one of them?" he finally asked, his voice breaking on the last word.

"No." Now Jez was smiling. "Oh, hell no." She glanced around the room. "I just have this, uh, *friend* who was there with Abigail last month."

A picture began to form in Walter's mind.

Her voice was a little lower. "You remember when we first met, in the wood store, next to the magazine rack?"

He nodded.

"That wasn't by happenstance," she said.

Walter felt dizzy. He placed both hands on the sides of his head.

"Hey," Jez said, her voice quick with concern. "Ease up, friend. Just relax for a minute. I didn't mean to freak you out."

They sat silently for a long time, their eyes meeting. Walter was breathing heavily. He finally managed to speak, "I was trying to convince myself that that didn't happen."

"I happened to meet them," she said, "pretty much the way you did."

"Them." Walter frowned.

She chuckled. "I don't know how to refer to them. I can't tell if it's one, uh, *person* or if there *are* even individuals."

Walter looked down at his coffee cup. "It did seem to be an individual in Abigail. No gender that I could tell." He thought of how that evening went, of tutoring Abigail, but then of having her suddenly on top of him, tugging at his belt.

"My friend," she said, "has the appearance of a man, younger than you. He has told me that he's not male or female, but it's really hard to keep from thinking of him as *him*." Then suddenly she touched Walter's hand. "You mustn't tell anyone about them."

"You just told me."

"I was asked to. They trust you."

"Why?"

"I don't know," she said. "I guess because of how you were with Abigail."

Walter suddenly felt like crying. "Why me?" He took a deep breath and let it out slowly. He felt something that was like grief, thinking about that woman, how he had taken care of her, not knowing that it was not a *she* at all. For a few hours, he had cared for someone in a way he'd never done before. He couldn't remember his wife ever having been that vulnerable with him. Whatever that *being* was, in Abigail's apartment, Walter felt something for it, an empathy.

He drank the rest of his cold coffee. "What did they tell you about me?" Inside, he was squirming, but he needed to know.

Jez smiled at him. "Everything."

He hid his face in his hands and groaned.

"Understandable, Walter," she said quietly. "You didn't know."

He looked up at the gray-haired woman sitting across the table from him, suddenly feeling a connection. "How did you learn about them?" he asked.

"I was installing some kitchen cabinets in a new house, laying on my back with a screwdriver in my hand, and just shooting the shit with the fellow who was helping me." She grinned widely. "We got to talking about something, and it got to the subject of sex. You know, how guys talk."

Walter grinned back. This was an unusual woman.

"Well, I said that I'd never felt comfortable with sex. I wasn't against it, but I didn't understand what all the fuss was about. And this fellow leaned over so I could see his face through the openings in the cabinet, and he said, 'I don't either.' We both howled."

Walter had to laugh at that.

"Then after we got off work," she said, "we went to a bar for a drink. Well, I'm a cheap date. I can't hold much liquor." She spread her arms out wide. "I ain't very big, after all. But anyway I was pretty relaxed, n'he and I got into some pretty serious talk, n'then he lowered his voice and told me that he wasn't who he looked to be."

"Was it somebody who died?" The image came to him of Abigail sitting in the car, looking scared.

"I guess that's how they work," she said.

"They can take somebody who just died, and fix them so they function again?"

"The thing is, it has to be somebody who is pretty isolated. Otherwise, there'd be all these relationships they'd have to deal with."

"Abigail didn't seem to have many relationships, except for that one guy." Walter sighed. "When he came there and found her dead, he was really shook up."

"I found my dad two years ago," she said quietly, "on the floor of his shop. I had nobody to call. My mom died years ago."

"No brothers or sisters?"

"No."

"Sorry for your loss," he said, at a loss for words.

"Thank you."

"What do you think they want?" Walter asked.

"Just to watch us, I think. They don't know anything about human emotions or relationships or stuff like that. They're just in their heads—so to speak."

They both laughed.

"My friend is really curious about sex," Jez said, smiling.

Walter lowered his voice. "You say they told you everything."

She nodded, that smile of conspiracy on her face.

He looked down. "It was like the woman had just discovered how to do it. She didn't hesitate, she just went for it, like she'd been doing it all along."

"Probably Abigail had."

He looked down. "I hadn't done it in six years."

"But you still knew how."

He laughed. Then he sighed. "Woke something up in me."

"This is a very weird conversation," Jez said.

"Isn't it."

"Will you talk to him?"

"Your friend?"

"Nothing to worry about," she said. "He's a pussy cat."

"Lemme think about it."

Walter waited another week before calling Jez. "I don't know what they expect from me," he said.

"Don't worry."

"This is very weird."

"You can do it. All they want is to talk with you—about yourself."

Walter blurted, "Am I going to die, and they want my body?"

Jez laughed, longer than Walter was comfortable with it. "Relax, friend. No, they don't want your body." Then she added an afterthought: "I don't think."

"Jez, I want to be straight with you," he said. "There's a part of me that's curious as hell. And another part that's scared shitless."

"Yep."

"I feel like I'm in way over my head."

"Yep."

He laughed. "You are something else, you know it?"

"Never was much of a standard model."

"It's like I can say anything to you."

"Might as well."

"What's that mean?" Holding his phone with a hunched-up shoulder, Walter was toying with a carpenter's pencil, creating a shaded drawing on a blueprint.

"You don't owe me anything. I ain't never going to be your lover."

"It's like you're a friend, and I don't even know you."

"You want to just forget this whole thing?"

"Too late."

"Okay, can you come to my place about five?"

Walter took a deep breath. "Okay."

She hung up without another word.

Later, he sat in his car, still in front of his house. *I'm gonna die,* he thought. *I'm in the middle of a thing like that movie with Scarlett Johansson, 'Under the Skin'. Jez is a real Jezebel, leading me to my death.*

But he laughed, thinking about how different Jez was from Scarlett Johansson. *Abigail might have gotten me with sex, but not this butch woman. Wonder if she's ever ..."*

He started the car.

Walter pulled into the driveway and parked behind two pickup trucks. Jez's truck was old and rusted; the other one a late-model, clean and unblemished. He went to the back door—it seemed more appropriate in an old place like this.

Jez smiled at him when she opened the door. "Knew you'd come," she said. "We're in the parlor."

"Walter, meet Freddy." She gestured to Walter to sit in an overstuffed chair.

Freddy looked young, maybe about thirty, short scruffy beard, hair just a little long. A journeyman, used to working with his hands. Jeans torn at the knees. His chambray shirt had never been ironed since it was new. "Hi, Walter," he said in a slight Tennessee accent. There was nothing about this man to reveal how different he actually was.

Walter didn't know what to say. He waited for Jez to break the ice.

"Walter is just a little bit anxious," she said finally.

"I need some help," said Freddy. "Jez thinks you might be able to help me."

"I'm about to freak out," Walter admitted, "but I'll hear what you have to say."

"I'm here to learn about people. We don't mean no harm to anybody."

Walter frowned. "First I need to know about you. I've already met one of your kind, and that went all right."

Freddy smiled. "One of us, you say."

"Well, didn't I?"

"I guess you could say that."

Jez spoke up, "I say 'they' a lot, but I think it's more complicated than that."

"I think I'm in over my head," said Walter.

"No you're not," said Jez, "no more'n me."

"Jez calls me 'him' a lot," said Freddy. "That's okay, if it makes it any easier for you. You know that 'male' and 'female' are strange concepts for us. Abigail told you that we all come from a single 'song'. Songs spring from us and grow into new individuals."

Walter frowned. "That's what she said."

"It's the closest word we know in English to how we multiply." Those words, coming out in that Tennessee accent, seemed very strange. "We appear to you in these separate forms—these bodies—in order to communicate better with you."

Jez laughed. "That's how Freddy and I connected in the beginning—neither of us understands what sex is all about."

"I'm sure no expert," said Walter, resting a hand on his knee to stop its shaking. "In school I learned about how sexual activity is only one way life replicates itself on Earth. It seems to work pretty good." He chuckled. "Works for me, although I don't have any children."

Freddy smiled. "It was very interesting, when it happened between you and Abigail."

Walter felt his neck becoming warm. He cleared his throat. "Well, since you know all about that already," and he looked quickly at Jez, "Abigail was very—"

"Sexy?" asked Jez.

He nodded, blushing.

"Would a child grow from that action, if Abigail had not been allowed to die?" Freddy sat hunched forward, elbows on his knees, watching Walter carefully.

"You just let her die? Just like that?" Walter felt anger rising inside him. At the same time, he was aware of a strange mixture of emotions, thinking about Abigail.

"She had already died," Freddy said gently. "We let her go because her heart was very damaged. She would not have lived long. She was the wrong vehicle for us."

Walter took a deep breath and let it out. "Not every sexual act results in children." He was aware that he was trying to keep from talking about sex and Abigail.

"It seemed to be a very intense experience for both of you."

Walter scratched his head, trying to find words. "Yes, sometimes it is."

After a moment of silence, he looked up at Freddy and said, "You said 'we.' You've been saying 'we' but you said—the way I heard it—you're not separate individuals."

Freddy grinned. "It's to make it easier for you. When I say 'I' it's mostly to refer to this body, that you know as Freddy."

"Then there's something else," Walter said. "When I was with Abigail, she said, 'I wish I were Abigail.' Was that you?"

Freddy ran his fingers through his hair. "The feeling was Abigail's." To Walter's look of bewilderment, he added, "Emotions and feelings are strange to us."

"Song—you used the word 'song' as though it meant something very special to you. Isn't that emotion?"

Jez laughed, and looked at Freddy. "See, didn't I tell you?"

Walter's mind kept jumping around among the three or four different feelings he was experiencing. Finally, he said what he really wanted to know: "Okay, here it is—what do you plan to do here? Are you going to take over the Earth and kill us all, or turn us into your herd of animals, or simply occupy our bodies and perform some kind of theater play?"

Freddy smiled again. "You seem to be tense."

"Goddamn right I'm tense! I don't know how all this is going to turn out."

"We're here just to observe you."

"What's your objective?"

"Interesting," Freddy said, in a tone like a college professor watching an experiment run. "Freddy is feeling something, an arousal."

"Christ!" Walter almost shouted. "That's what you said when you were in Abigail!"

Jez looked quickly at him. "I think Freddy is reacting to your anger."

Suddenly embarrassed, Walter slumped back in the chair. His memory of Abigail, her vulnerability, almost sweet innocence, played through his mind. He saw her touch her abdomen with a kind of curiosity. And then she had said softly, "I know what the feeling is now."

He shook his head. "It's too much. I can't deal with it." He stood up and looked at Jez. "Do you get it, Jez?"

She smiled. "It's something, isn't it?"

"Do you know what they are doing here?" He turned to Freddy. "How many of you are there?"

Freddy seemed perplexed. "You mean—"

"How many bodies are you inhabiting right now?"

"No human is being harmed. We're just here to observe."

"I don't believe you!" Walter turned and left the house. In his car, he took a deep breath and let it out before starting the engine. *What kinda shit am I into? I can't believe this! How come I'm the one they picked to question? They could be just leading us on, and in*

*the end will end us all! If they are anything, they are
not like us.*

W alter went to work the next week feeling as
though the world was going to end very soon,
but he didn't know what to do with the
feelings. He tried hard to keep focused on his work, as
though if he could ignore the situation, it wasn't really
there.

But at lunch with Charlie and Shep, he had to say
something: "You know that thing I talked about, that
woman I found on the highway?"

Shep and Charlie stopped eating and stared at
him. "You mean your alien visitor?" asked Shep, a
grin on his face.

"You're still convinced, are you?" said Charlie.

"Had another experience," Walter said, and
briefly described his meeting Jez and Freddy.

"Holy shit!" said Charlie.

"They're here," Walter said. "They could be all
around us. You can't tell by looking at them." He
sighed quickly. "And it may not even be 'them.' I
couldn't get straight whether it's one huge being, with
just parts occupying separate humans, or if it's a lot
of them. The ones I talked to seemed to be the same,
uh, person or whatever it is."

"You mean the same alien in the woman and in
the man?"

"They're not used to the whole idea of different
sexes. They kept asking me how that works." Walter

still couldn't admit to his friends that he had had sex with Abigail.

Shep laughed. "Didn't you offer to demonstrate?"

Charlie was frowning. "I wouldn't be able to get it up for an alien—creeps me out just thinking about it."

"You say they could be all around us," said Shep. "What are they up to?"

"Don't have a clue. Freddy and Abigail both said they mean us no harm."

"Wonder if the government knows about them," Charlie said.

"Probably do," Shep answered, "but they wouldn't tell us because everybody'd panic."

"Maybe we *should* panic," said Walter, staring at his uneaten sandwich. "I don't know what to do."

"You said the woman had died, and they just took over her body and brought her back to life," said Charlie. "How'd they get inside Freddy?"

"I didn't ask." Walter picked up his sandwich. "He pissed me off."

"You got pissed?" Shep thought that was funny. "You pull out your ray gun and threaten to zap him?"

Walter shook his head and took a bite. "When he saw I was angry, he got a little hot himself."

"Shootout at the OK Corral," laughed Shep.

I'm not laughin'," said Charlie. "We could be facing the end of the world or something."

Walter shrugged.

"We better get back to work," said Shep, "or we won't have jobs to go to—in case the world doesn't end."

As the three of them left the restaurant, Shep said, "You know how they always ask—if you know you're going to die in a short time, what would you want to be doing in the meantime."

"Ain't funny," muttered Charlie.

That afternoon Walter sat in his cubicle, thinking. *I don't think those guys really believe this. I'm not sure I believe it myself. If it's true, we could be in deep shit. But what the hell can we do? Freddy and his kind have all the cards. They know what they're doing, and we don't.*

By the time he got off work, he felt resigned to whatever was going to happen. But he had to know. He would get in touch with Jez again.

"Thought you might have skipped out," she said when he phoned her.

"No place to hide," he said.

Jez laughed. "If you spend more time with Freddy you might feel easier."

"I mean it—I can't hide. I can't walk away. I have to know what's going to happen."

"They pegged you right, didn't they?"

"What's that mean?" The conversation was making Walter nervous.

"You have integrity."

He was silent.

"Can you meet him tomorrow evening? At my place?"

"All right."

The next day Walter pulled into Jez's drive and parked behind the two pickup trucks. He let himself into her house without knocking, and found them in the parlor as before. He sat in the same overstuffed chair and waited.

"I'm glad you came," said Freddy.

Jez simply smiled at him.

"What do you want from me?" Walter asked, his voice subdued.

"Tell me about love," said Freddy.

"What?" Walter was startled. He had half-expected questions about sex, about male and female creating new humans by copulating. Physical mating. Biology.

Freddy leaned forward, his elbows on his knees. "You are one human, and I need your individual view. Others, we know, have different points of view. I need only yours. Tell me what love means to you."

Walter cleared his throat. "I'm not any expert."

"I know that." Freddy waited.

"I'm not a very good subject for that question. I was married until six years ago, when my wife left me."

"Did you love her?"

"Yes." Walter sighed. "I think I still do."

"But you hate her, too, don't you?" said Jez.

Walter looked over at the woman. He started to say something, then stopped.

"Is love related to hate?" asked Freddy.

"For me," Walter began, "love is feeling strongly pulled toward someone else, wanting to be near that person, willing to give up other things, other people." He stopped, frowning. "That sounds so shallow! Love is deep."

Suddenly Walter felt something rise up in his throat. He thought of Daniele, and his old grief gripped him again as though all that were just yesterday.

"What—" Freddy began, but Walter stopped him with a gesture.

He took a deep breath. His voice grating, he said, "It's like the other person is a part of you. She completes you. And at the same time you are willing to give up everything else for her sake." He was thinking about Daniele, picturing her in her favorite chair, smiling at him, open to him—totally vulnerable to him.

"You are feeling something," Freddy said quietly. Freddy was suddenly the therapist, coaxing it out of him.

It was too intense for Walter. He cleared his throat. "Of course there are different kinds of love," he said. "Love for your children, love for your parents, for good friends, for mankind."

Freddy smiled. "You shifted. You're not talking about yourself."

"It's been six years," Walter sighed. "I thought I was over her—the dependency part."

Jez said, "Love is taking and giving."

"Yes."

"You said you still love her," said Freddy.

Walter smiled wryly. "That's the giving part. That's easy, once the hurt is healed. Forgiveness."

"The taking part is what hurts?"

Walter looked at him. "I thought you said you didn't know anything about love."

"We're learning."

"So am I," said Jez.

Walter turned to her. "And you said you didn't understand love."

"I said sex," she answered. I do know about love— a little."

"You know about loss?"

Her face was serious. "You betcha."

Walter was beginning to pick up something from Jez. The image he'd had, of this "butch woman" had been too simple. "Tell me."

"He was my god," she said.

He waited for more.

"He taught me everything I knew. When my mom died, he was all I had." She took a deep breath and let it out. "Then he died."

"I'm sorry."

"He loved me," she said, looking out the window, "he gave me all he could, but he couldn't know all the time what I needed."

"Maybe that's why Daniele left," Walter said. "I couldn't give her everything she needed."

Freddy looked at Walter. "How do you do it, you humans? How do you know what others have in their minds?"

Jez chuckled. "Not a problem for you, is it?"

Freddy looked at her questioningly.

"You are not separate like we are," she said.

Walter turned to Freddy, "We have to do it just like we're doing it here, right now. We talk. We touch. We use body language."

"Body language?"

"It's how you hold yourself with someone else," Jez explained, "how you gesture, your facial expressions."

"The last time we were together," Freddy said to Walter, "I felt something from you. I couldn't describe it in words, but then you expressed anger—pretty clearly."

Jez laughed. "That he did."

"That feeling I had then. How did that happen?"

Walter scratched his head. "I've read that we are very good at reading each other. I guess that's what you felt. You were picking up subtle vibes—I don't know what to call it, exactly. Vibes—vibrations—is what some people call it.

"And all that happens whenever people are together?"

"Some people close themselves off so you can't read them, and some people aren't good at reading." Walter watched Freddy, wondering how much of this he understood.

"When you were with Abigail," Freddy said, holding Walter's gaze, "it was more than simple physical connecting, wasn't it?"

Walter blushed. "You dig deep, don't you?"

Jez laughed.

Freddy furrowed his brow. "You were vibrating?"

That made both Walter and Jez laugh out loud.

"I was, indeed. Good sex always includes good vibes." He took a breath and looked at Jez. "I can't believe I'm talking like this to a stranger."

"You're not closed," said Freddy.

"When you were in Abigail," Walter began, then paused. "You *were* in Abigail, weren't you?"

Freddy smiled.

Walter looked across the room, anywhere except at Freddy. "It's hard to get my mind around all that."

"Wow," said Jez softly.

"When you were in Abigail, you said, 'I wish I were Abigail.' And yet you say you don't know about emotions. I wanted to ask you the other day about that. You said humans have emotions, as though you don't."

Freddy looked at him without speaking.

"Wasn't that emotion?"

"I don't know. Something."

Walter opened his hands, as though to open the idea. "It's like people—people I know, anyway—communicate on different levels at the same time. The top level, the superficial level, is the words they use and the deliberate body language. The words you can look up in the dictionary to find out what they mean."

He paused. "Under that level can be a number of levels of meaning. Deeper meaning. Like irony, for example. Irony is a meaning that can be the opposite of the top level of meaning. I can say to you, 'You are an honorable man' but mean that I think you are not honorable. It's only effective if the person being addressed understands the deeper meaning. If you have just cheated someone, and I say that you are honorable, both of us know it isn't true." Walter looked at Freddy. "Does that make sense to you?"

Freddy was silent for a moment. "No," he said finally.

"Beneath that layer of meaning could be other layers. I might say those words to you and be quoting someone else, who said them to someone else, with reference to some other situation. If we both know about that other situation and that statement that I've quoted, it might mean something even deeper."

"I'm trying to understand."

"It takes years to learn these things," Walter said. "You can't be expected to learn them easily. You need a lot of experiences to integrate such knowledge."

"I'm trying to understand, too," Jez said. "You're over my head."

Walter smiled. "Jez just said I was over her head. That's another figure of speech, which means something different from the dictionary meaning of the words. It means that what I just described is beyond her understanding."

"You're over my head," said Freddy.

They all laughed.

"I don't know what else to say," said Walter. "When you first revealed yourself to me, you said you were here—or there, in Abigail—to observe. I don't know what else to tell you."

Jez, looking at Freddy, said, "In the beginning, I thought you were super-intelligent, you knew everything, but I'm beginning to think you're short a thing or two."

Freddy laughed. "I get your figure of speech. You mean we need to learn a lot more than 'a thing or two'."

"Bingo," said Jez.

Walter stood up. "There are a lot of people who are a lot wiser than I am. You need to contact them."

Freddy was silent.

"Freddy," said Jez, "tell me something?"

"You mean, you're asking me to tell you something—right?"

She grinned at him. "How did you get into Freddy?"

"He was electrocuted. He touched an electric wire while working at his trade."

"And in that instant, you took over." She pursed her lips, thinking.

"Yes."

"He must have been an all right guy."

"I don't know." Freddy looked thoughtful.

"What will happen to his body?"

"He will be found. Someone will take him away."

"Feels weird," she said.

"That's how it's done," said Walter. "You said we will not be harmed."

"Yes."

"Then I am going back to my life." he said, starting for the door.

Jez followed him. "You haven't showed me your shop," she said quietly.

He turned to her. "You're in my life—if you want to be."

She put a hand on his arm. "I do want to be."

"Good." Then he raised his voice. "Good bye, Freddy."

"Thank you, Walter," he said in that strange Tennessee accent.

Walter went to his truck and backed out of the drive.

Three

M ichael looked up from the desk. She was pretty and slim, even though, to him, a little "older."

She held out a coupon. "I'm Abby DeVoe," she said. "I understand this gives me a discount on five visits to your gym."

"Indeed it does," he said, pulling a paper from a drawer. "Would you fill out this application form?"

After the paperwork was finished, Michael showed Abby around the workout room, demonstrating each machine. On those that required adjustments, he had her try out the machine herself, and wrote down the appropriate numbers for her.

"I'm not on the staff here," he told her. "I'm just filling in for the secretary while she's at lunch. But I'm pretty much a regular here. I come a lot of evenings after work, and usually on Saturdays. I like how my body feels after a workout."

"I know I should take better care of my body," she said. "That's why I'm here."

"Well, anytime I can help you, just let me know."

After seeing each other at the gym occasionally, they began to chat more, and sometimes went out for coffee together before heading home. In time, friendship developed.

He'd never met a woman like Abby. Vivacious and impulsive, she acted much younger than she looked, but she was also thoughtful, unlike most of the women his own age, whom he thought to be often frivolous and empty. Their conversations were about important things, like climate change and the Middle East, and how individuals could cope with the fast pace of the world.

She was an editor in a small magazine publishing company. "All day I read about farm equipment, but my heart is in poetry."

"You write poetry?"

She laughed. "A little, but nothing I want to show to anybody."

"I have to admit that I don't understand most poetry I've read. I like to read short fiction—stories that don't get too mysterious."

After several months, the two became intimate, usually going to her apartment after dinner together. Occasionally, he slept over.

"You said you like gin," she said one evening, going to the pantry. "I bought some tonic water, too."

"Terrific." He stood in the doorway, watching her.

"I don't like to drink alone." She took down two glasses and filled them with ice from the refrigerator. Turning to look at him, she said, "Sometimes I get depressed, and that's a bad time to drink alcohol."

"Yes," he said. "Why do you get depressed?"

She smiled. "I don't know. I don't often have company here, in spite of the fact that I get lonely sitting in there watching television.

As she poured gin into the glasses, he said, "If you keep the gin in the freezer, you can enjoy just a quick shot once in a while to pick you up." He laughed. "Especially that Bombay Sapphire."

She smiled. "Is this good gin?"

"Very good."

She handed him a drink and they touched glasses. "Thank you," he said.

In the next few weeks, their evenings in her apartment became more and more sexual. Abby was quite enthusiastic as a lover, and Michael was delighted.

Michael emptied the glass of wine he'd been nursing, and looked around the room. The other diners were laughing and chatting together, most having finished their meals and were preparing to leave.

Abby had never been this late. They alternated their dinner locations between Braille, where she lived, and the city, his home territory, since there were few restaurants in between them that they liked. Ever since they had become close, they talked about one of them moving nearer, but their jobs were important to both of them.

He looked at his watch. She'd suggested this restaurant for tonight because of the atmosphere. But she was an hour late. He phoned her apartment. There was no answer. *On her way,* he guessed. He promised himself that he would try to persuade her to buy a cell phone, something that she had insisted was "too technical" for her.

Michael ordered another glass of Chardonnay and waited. He'd already looked at the menu and chosen what he would eat, but didn't order anything, nibbling on the bread the waiter had brought.

After the second glass of wine, he tried her phone again. This time a man answered.

Startled, Michael hesitated. "May I speak with Abigail?"

The man sounded older. "She can't come to the phone right now. Do you know Abigail?"

Michael hesitated. "Yes. She and I were supposed to meet this evening."

"What's your name?"

"Michael. Abigail and I were supposed to meet at eight o'clock, and she hasn't shown up yet. Is she there? Is she all right?"

The man's tone worried Michael, "I think it might be good if you came here."

Michael felt foreboding rising up inside. "What's wrong? Who are you?"

"Please come." And the phone clicked off.

His heart pounding, he signaled the waiter for the check, paid and immediately left the restaurant.

On the drive to Braille, he tried to remember if Abby had other men friends. Who would that be at her apartment? The guy hadn't said she was or was not there, only that she couldn't come to the phone. A policeman or emergency worker would surely have identified himself.

By the time Michael knocked on her door, he was shaking with apprehension.

A strange man opened the door and, apparently knowing who Michael was, pointed to the bedroom. "She's in there," he said simply. "She died in her sleep."

Michael rushed into the bedroom, where Abby lay on top of the covers, appearing as though she were asleep. He felt her neck for a pulse. All his fear boiled up into sobbing grief, and he threw himself on her body. He wasn't even aware that the man slipped out without saying anything. Later, Michael found a note that told where to find Abby's car on the highway from the city. Her keys were with the note.

How did she die? Who was that man? Why didn't he stay and explain anything? What should I do? Michael sat down in Abby's living room to collect himself.

Finally, he decided that he had to report this to the police. He dialed 9-1-1.

While the emergency crew collected Abby's body and wheeled it down to the EMS vehicle, two plainclothes policemen questioned Michael. He told them everything he knew, and showed them the note.

"Do you know where this is?" asked one, pointing to the note.

"Yes, approximately," Michael answered.

"We'll run out there and see. Are those her keys to the car?"

"Yes, I think so."

"These other two keys—do you know what they are to?"

Michael pulled his own keys out of his pocket and compared one to Abigail's keys. "This one is her apartment." He gestured toward the door. "The other one, I don't know. Maybe it's to her storage locker in the basement."

"I don't see any evidence of foul play," said one detective. "But we need you to be available for more questions, okay?"

"Sure." He gave them his business card from work.

"Okay, you can go. When we find out anything, we'll let you know."

Driving back home, Michael felt only sadness. Abby had become such a close friend—and lover.

Approaching the city, he saw flashing lights ahead, and recognized Abby's car already being loaded onto a carrier. He didn't stop.

The next day, he phoned the Braille police and asked about the investigation. They told him that Abby had in all likelihood suffered a heart attack. The emergency room in the city had told them that she had been brought in by a man who then left with her, apparently to take her to her home. Everything fit together, and it was being treated as a "natural causes" case. They wanted to talk with the man who had brought her to the E.R. They said they had his name and address.

For days, Michael couldn't stop thinking about Abby. They hadn't gotten to the stage in their relationship where they talked about the future, but he had often thought of her with feelings that approached love. He hadn't been in a romantic relationship for some time, and she offered him both comfort and excitement.

She hadn't revealed much about her past, and the single photograph on her piano showed an elderly couple who she said were her parents. With his phone, Michael had taken a selfie of the two of them, and had it printed and framed for her. The next time he had visited, the picture was on the piano next to her parents.

The gym seemed haunted. Every time a woman came in, he looked, half expecting it to be Abby.

He called the Braille police, asking about her, and about the strange man who had been in her apartment that night. On the phone, they seemed reluctant to tell him much, so one day he took off work and drove there to talk to someone in person.

"He was the one who had taken her into the E.R.," they told him. "We interviewed him, and he seemed straightforward, a good Samaritan who saw her on the highway and stopped to help. He said he didn't want to get involved—that's why he left when you arrived."

They also said that they had tracked down her mother, who was in a nursing home in Battle Creek. Her Alzheimer's prevented her from giving much information. The officer smiled. "Your mystery woman is still pretty much a mystery," she said.

"Can you give me the number of the man?" Michael asked. "At least I'd like to thank him for taking care of her."

"Can't do that," she said, but opened the file on her desk and half-turned it. "Excuse me," she said, "I have to get something from the back office."

When she left the room, Michael looked at the open file and wrote on a scrap of paper "Walter Anderson" and the phone number. When the officer returned, he thanked her and left.

❧—❧

A n answering machine met his call. He left his name and number without explaining why he'd called.

A week later, Michael answered his own phone to hear, "This is Walter Anderson. You called me last week."

"Yes," Michael said, "I've been wanting to talk with you about Abigail DeVoe."

"I don't know her," Walter said, and hung up.

Michael called his number again. After four rings, Walter answered.

"I don't mean to cause you any trouble," Michael said. "I talked with the Braille police, and they said they had talked with you but didn't think there was any problem."

"They did talk with me, and I told them everything I knew," Walter said. "I just found her sitting in her car and I took her to her home."

"They also said you took her to the emergency room. I'm grateful for that."

"What's your connection with Abigail?"

"Just good friends," Michael said.

There was a long pause in the conversation. Then Michael asked, "You were with her when she died?"

"Yes."

"Uh—was she in any pain?"

"Not that I could tell. It was quite sudden. The doctors said she had a heart condition."

"Why didn't you stay long enough to just tell me what had happened?"

"I was a stranger. I didn't want to get involved."

Michael was silent for a moment. Then he said, "She wanted to write poetry."

It was Walter's turn to be silent. "Do you want to meet for coffee?"

"I'd like that," Michael said.

"There's a Denny's downtown on High Street. Do you know where that is?"

Walter recognized the young man immediately. He signaled to him.

After they had seated themselves in a booth, Walter said, "I guess you're curious about me. I'm curious about Abigail."

He explained that he had taken her home, but when he went into the bathroom, she apparently lay down on the bed and just died there. When he emerged from the bathroom, she showed no sign of life.

Michael sagged visibly.

"The E.R. recommended that she see her regular doctor as soon as possible," Walter said. "I guess it was more serious than they thought."

The two men sat silently for a time.

Then Walter said, "When you called, she seemed to be kind of out of it, like she wasn't functioning very well. I thought she should have someone there who knew her, at least. I didn't know what to do for her."

"Yeah," said Michael. "When you left, I was really confused. I didn't know her parents or anything. I thought the best thing was to report it to the police."

"She seemed like a nice woman." Walter thought about that night, as he had slowly realized that Abigail was not really Abigail, and he had felt completely lost. "I was glad you called—at least you knew who she was."

"I've never had to deal with a situation like that," Michael said. "I've never even seen a dead person except my grandmother, when I was a kid."

Walter wanted to tell this young man about Abigail, the Abigail he had encountered the night she had died, but there seemed no way it could make any sense. Even now, he had a hard time trying to understand what had happened.

"She seemed confused," he said, "the whole evening. I guess she had a stroke, and it took away some of her mental capacity."

"Her mind was always so sharp," Michael said.

"Have you tried to find out if she had any family?"

"No." He screwed up his face. "I thought we were really close, but she never mentioned her family. There was just one photo in her apartment—but I guess you saw that—of her parents, I guess."

"Probably the police would try to locate them. They'd go through her things to find out."

"Thanks for talking with me, at least. You were kind of a mystery man."

Walter pushed his coffee spoon around on the table. "The police called me, but I couldn't tell them anything except what I've told you. They didn't seem concerned about me."

Michael put his elbows on the table, his hands clasping his coffee cup. "I don't mean to raise any questions or put you on the spot, but—"

Walter looked up, surprised.

"There were a couple of glasses on the coffee table, and some frozen food containers in the kitchen." He gave a little nervous laugh. "I gather that you two had something to eat and drink. You didn't mention that."

Walter looked at him for a moment, then said, "I was trying to get through to her. I thought she might be hungry. We both ate."

"I'm surprised that she ate that. She was a vegetarian."

Walter took a deep breath. "She didn't say anything." He was getting uncomfortable.

"She had both meat and veggie dishes in the freezer, 'cause I eat meat. But she never did, that I know of." Michael was looking intently at Walter.

Walter shrugged. "She didn't seem to know how to eat." Then he stopped, regretting what he'd just said. "I mean, maybe she was confused."

"I keep thinking that there's something you aren't telling me." Michael leaned on one elbow.

Walter was now very uncomfortable. "Uh, I can't think of anything more. We went to her apartment and I was trying to find out if I could call anybody for her. Then you called, and I thought you could handle it."

"And you both had gin and tonics," Michael said. "The gin bottle was out on the table, and she always keeps it in the freezer. The glasses still had ice in them."

Walter remembered that evening, when he had to show Abigail how to drink. She seemed so innocent then, almost as though she were in a dream. Then he remembered, for the hundredth time, how she had jumped on him and begun loosening his belt. His face felt hot.

"I don't mean to put you on the spot," said Michael, "but maybe I do. Was she drunk? Did you get her drunk?" He sat back in his seat. "Did you tell me to come there because she had passed out drunk?"

"No!" Walter felt anger rising, and the hair on the back of his neck stood up. "Wouldn't the autopsy show that?"

"They didn't let me see the autopsy report," said Michael.

"Well, they sure didn't ask me such a question."

Michael looked down. "I'm sorry," he said. "I just feel like there's something more to this. I guess I'm just paranoid. I'm sorry."

Walter took a breath. "Yeah, I fixed us both a gin and tonic. It wasn't even very strong. Couldn't have had anything to do with her death. I don't think."

Michael's eyes were misting up. "I'm sorry," he said softly. "I miss her—a lot."

Walter relaxed a little. "I understand. I only knew her for an hour or so. She seemed a nice person, but she was obviously very ill."

"She never told me anything about a heart condition. She worked out on the machines at the gym, and seemed to handle that pretty well."

Walter sighed. Then he looked directly at Michael. "I may regret this," he said quietly. And then he told the other man what had happened that night—everything except the sex.

Michael, at first, returned Walter's gaze with widening eyes. Then gradually his face betrayed a growing anger. "I don't know what you think you're doing," he said. "I don't believe any of that shit!"

Walter sighed again. "Yeah. It was a mistake. Forget the whole thing."

Both men got up from the booth and left the restaurant without exchanging another word. Walter stopped at the cashier stand and paid for the coffee. By the time he reached his car, Michael had gone.

The coroner of Braille County eventually issued a report on the death of Abigail DeVoe, calling it a heart attack.

The police notified the manager of the condo where she had lived that her unit could be cleaned out for another resident. The manager hired a local auction company to come in and remove everything. It was taken temporarily to a garage-type storage unit.

A month later, Walter got a flyer in the mail announcing an auction at a storage facility. The flyer had been mailed in a plain business envelope with no return address. In the list of lockers to be auctioned off, one unit had been circled with a felt-tip pen. Walter almost threw it away before noticing that the zip code on the envelope was that of Braille.

Curious, he looked up the location of the storage facility. It was just outside the town of Braille.

For two days, he left the flyer on his desk at home. Then he picked it up, intending to throw it into the trash until he noticed that the auction was to be that day. Instead of discarding it, he pocketed the flyer and drove to Braille.

The contents of six units in the little facility were to be auctioned off. No one was allowed to enter past the yellow tape across each open door.

A small crowd of people had gathered for the auctions, drifting back and forth along the line of units and peering into the interiors, some with flashlights.

Walter identified the unit that had been circled on his flyer, and looked inside at a collection of boxes and furniture. Nothing caught his attention. It was simply a bunch of unremarkable junk, somebody's belongings that had not been worth paying for the monthly charges. Only two or three people took any interest in the unit.

He waited until the auctioneer got to that unit to begin the sale. "What can you tell me about this one?" he asked.

The auctioneer seemed uninterested. "All I can tell you is somebody died, and nobody claimed their stuff."

Walter got up as close as the tape would allow and peered into the unit again. In the back, behind a stack of boxes, stood a small piano. Someone else was standing alongside him, and noticed the piano at the same time. "There's a boat anchor for you," he said. "Can't give those things away these days." The man walked away, but Walter continued to stare at the piano. *That was in Abigail's apartment,* he thought. *These were her belongings!*

The mysterious flyer, with the storage unit number circled, suddenly became meaningful. Someone had sent it to him because these things belonged to Abigail. His heart pounded. He didn't dwell on the question of who had sent the flyer—the important thing was that he needed to see what her apartment had held.

When the auctioneer began the litany, Walter made the first bid. Only two other people bid, and when he had raised the bid to a hundred dollars, both of them dropped out.

"You got four days to get this stuff out of here," the auctioneer told him as an assistant took Walter's money, name and address. "Every bit of it has to be out of here by, uh, next Wednesday. Otherwise, we will remove it and bill you for the transportation to the landfill."

Although he wanted to explore the contents of the storage unit he had just purchased, Walter didn't want to do it so publicly. He obtained a padlock from the storage facility manager, and after securing the unit he went back home.

The next morning, he returned to the storage unit. Carefully sorting through the boxes, he separated Abigail's clothing and kitchen ware, all of which he would give to Goodwill Industries. What he was most interested in were the boxes of personal papers and books. These he put into two small boxes and carried them to his truck, along with a small end table that looked good enough to refinish.

On his way back home, he stopped at a small church near the storage facility. Several people stood around outside, evidently socializing after the Sunday service.

"Would you be interested in obtaining as a gift a small spinet-style piano?" he asked.

The men talked among themselves, and finally said that they might want it, if it was in good condition.

Walter drove two of the men back to the storage unit, where they agreed to take the piano off his hands if they could load it into his truck right then. Satisfied, Walter drove back home with his boxes, wondering what they would tell him.

At home, with papers scattered around the living room, he began to construct a picture of the woman to whom he had become somehow attached.

Abigail lived what appeared to be an austere life. Her equity in the condo was miniscule. No doubt the owner of the property would foreclose after a suitable time and re-sell it to someone else. She had a checking account containing less than a hundred dollars. A file folder contained a few receipts from retail stores.

Walter found an address book, but many of the entries had been crossed out, a few of which had other addresses penciled in. None appeared to be local except the nursing home where her mother lived.

A few letters from other people, dated years before, had been collected in a file folder. Nothing in them suggested close relationships.

Another file folder contained her condo contract, dated two years before, the title to her car and a legal document stapled together that certified that she had been divorced from a man named Henry DeVoe a dozen years before. The decree originated in Dallas, Texas.

A paper file portfolio contained typewritten documents, some of which were poems and others short stories, mostly unfinished. Penciled changes had been made on most of the documents.

Walter felt vaguely disappointed. He didn't know what he had expected, but Abigail DeVoe seemed to have been a lonely sort of woman, with few friends and, evidently, a mother with dementia her only living relative.

After dinner, he put on some music and settled down with the file folder of her writings. The one piece that caught his attention was a story or memoir:

                    Ian
              By Abigail Devoe

    Ian was a strange man. He was tall
and handsome, clean shaven but with long
sideburns, which reminded me of pictures
from the nineteenth century. We met as I
was bicycling through Mt. Airy Park in
the fall. The trees were turning, and
the air was cool.
    Ian was sitting on a park bench
alongside the trail. I stopped and we
exchanged pleasantries. "Just resting",
he said. He told me he had been walking,
but had just recovered from an injury
resulting from an automobile accident,
and he got tired easily. So we got into
a long conversation.
    At first I was uneasy with him
because he spoke so strangely, as though
he was speaking in a language foreign to
him. Yet he didn't seem to have an
accent, as most foreigners do. But after

a while I felt more comfortable because
he seemed friendly without prying.

I wondered if he had had brain injury
in his accident, which could have caused
his difficulties in speaking. You know
how sometimes you forget a word that is
familiar to you? Ian had a lot of those
words, except if I tried to help him by
suggesting words, he acted as though
he'd never known the words. Like
somebody from a foreign country.

He was intrigued with my bicycle,
wondering how it managed to stay upright
as I rode. I laughed, because bicycles
are so common—every child has one, at
some point in his or her life.

As we talked, he tried to tell me how
his people multiplied—through some kind
of "song". It was as though they didn't
have males and females.

I couldn't imagine where these people
might have lived. I've never heard of
any race that didn't multiply from
sexual intercourse.

After a while, I got a little nervous
around him. He was just too different,
even though he looked like an ordinary
person. I got on my bike and resumed my
ride. I never saw him again.

Ever since then, I've wondered

The writing stopped there, at the bottom of a
page. Walter thought that there must be more pages,
but they were not in the folder.

He went back and read the story again, feeling very strange. The way she described the man, it could have applied to her, that evening, as well. *Was Ian one of them? He must have been. When was that?* He couldn't shake the feeling, almost of *déjà vu.*

Most of the poems seemed to be just sketches, unfinished attempts of a beginning poet. One, however, revealed something else:

```
He thrusts inside me,
A wild animal
Who turns me into his kind.

We soar into the heaven
Together
Tasting ecstasy

And then deflated
Like children's balloons
To sleep in peace.
```

It reminded Walter again of that night. Something about Abigail had awakened him in ways he'd long forgotten.

Walter sighed, and closed the folder. *She knew,* he thought. *Or they knew her. She wrote that she never saw Ian again—but what about the poem?*

No, he decided, the poem could have been anybody. There were no dates on any of the pages.

Still. *What does it mean?*

The next day Walter took a sick day from work and drove his truck down to Braille, where he emptied out the storage unit, taking almost everything to a local Goodwill store. There was nothing else in the unit that interested him, even the photograph that had stood on her piano.

Jez's voice on the phone was somehow reassuring. "Hi, Friend," her message said. "I'm returning your call, and I'll be around the rest of today. Tomorrow I'm working at a construction site on the other side of town. You can get me in the evenings, though."

Walter, who had just gotten home from work, waited until after dinner before calling Jez back. "I've never showed you my shop," he told her. "When would you have time to come over and maybe share a dram or two?"

"I'll be pretty whacked out this week," she said, "with this site installation I'm doing. Can we make it next Sunday?"

"Perfect for me," he said. "Come for lunch. You still have my address?"

"Sure do. See you then."

That week Walter thought a lot about what he would say to Jez, and what she might say as well. He felt a kinship with her, and a trust that even though she was evidently in touch with *them*, she would respect his desire to avoid more contact with Freddy and his kind.

His discovery of Abigail's writing changed everything. How much of that was coincidence? That she might have had contact with one of them, and then when she died from a heart attack in her car, had they been observing her?

And who sent him that flyer about the storage facility auction? Was *he* being watched, even now?

On Friday after work, he debated whether to reveal any of this to Charlie and Shep. Jez had asked him not to say anything to others, although she didn't say why. But this was now a bigger thing than just Jez and Freddy.

"Why didn't you tell us you needed some help moving shit on Monday, Man?" Shep asked.

"Oh, I didn't know it was going to be so much. And a couple of guys from a church helped me with the piano."

"So what was all this stuff you had to move?" asked Charlie, tossing off his first shot of Patrón.

"Just some stuff in a storage locker that a friend couldn't pay any more to keep," Walter said.

"Where was this?"

Walter hesitated. "Braille."

"Braille," said Shep. "Isn't that where you were with that woman who died?"

"Was it her stuff?" asked Charlie.

Walter smiled. "Yeah."

"Didn't she have any relatives or anything to take care of it? Why you?"

Walter sighed. "I bought the contents of the storage unit," he admitted.

"You bought it?" Shep grinned. "Something you're not telling us about this babe? C'mon, Walter."

"I was just curious," said Walter.

"So did you turn up a hundred K stuffed in a mattress?"

"No, she didn't have anything of value," he lied.

"Man," said Charlie, "You've become something else since that shit went down. You're rattling on about aliens ..."

"And now you got a thing about a dead woman," added Shep.

The three were silent for a while, drinking tequila.

"You got any new ideas about these aliens?" asked Charlie.

"No."

"So they're not fixin' to take us down in the near future."

"I don't think so."

"Well," said Shep, "You'll let us know if we need to make our Last Will and Testament, right?"

Shep and Charlie exchanged glances.

Walter decided that there was nothing more to be said on the subject. Abigail's poem came up into his awareness for a moment—*these two guys would enjoy that poem*, he thought, *and understand nothing*.

Sunday morning Walter was nervous. He downed a straight shot of vodka to calm him down. He intended to show Abigail's writing to Jez, just so they could discuss the issues it brought up.

When she arrived, however, he first took her down to his basement shop. "You're a lot better equipped than I am," he said.

Jez looked over his machinery and his works in progress, and complimented him on his workmanship. She noticed the little end table he'd salvaged from Abigail's storage unit. "You didn't make that, though, did you?"

"No. I just thought I could refinish it."

"It's not up to your standards."

He laughed. "Thank you."

For lunch he made a mushroom omelet. As they ate, they chatted about woodworking.

Then he said, "I assume you're still in touch with Freddy."

She nodded without saying anything.

"I know I told you I didn't want to be involved with them anymore."

"Something's come up."

"Uh, yeah," he began, "you didn't send me a flyer from a storage facility, did you?"

She looked up quickly. "No."

"Somebody wanted me to know about the contents of Abigail's apartment."

She shook her head slowly, watching him.

"I was just curious about what she might have left," he said.

"And..."

"She must have been a pretty lonely person. There were almost no personal effects. But I bought the whole storage unit, and gave it away to a church and to Goodwill."

"Nothing you want to talk about?"

He went to his office and returned with the file folder. Without saying anything, he set it in front of her, and began clearing the table as she leafed through the pages.

"Lordy," she said, reading the memoir. Then she leafed through the poetry, pausing only momentarily at the erotic one.

Walter sat down across from her. "She knew about them," he said.

"Looks like it."

"Was she a marked woman?"

Jez looked up at him. "Do I think they did anything to her? No."

"But they knew her."

She shrugged. "I don't know what that would mean."

"Can't tell when these things were written," he said, gesturing toward the folder, "but maybe they had her under observation or something. Maybe the business when she had her heart attack in the car..." He stopped.

She shrugged again. "Man, you've got an active imagination."

"Aren't you curious?"

Jez grinned. "Not like you."

"I think they sent me that flyer so I would go to the storage locker."

She sat back in the chair and looked at him.

"Only people I've told about her is the Braille police, and they wouldn't be sending me a flyer."

"What about your friend Michael?"

"Oh, shit!" Walter slumped in his chair. "How do they know about him?"

She grinned again. "I guess they do have you in their field of vision."

"That doesn't bother you?"

Another shrug. "Okay, Freddy did tell me about Michael. They've been interested in him because of Abigail."

"So you know I've talked with him." A bead of sweat rolled down his temple.

"Yeah."

"He didn't believe me."

"Yeah."

Walter's brow furrowed. "Were they listening in to our conversation?"

She didn't reply.

"Jesus Christ! Now I am worried!"

Jez sat upright and looked directly at him. "They aren't here to harm anybody."

"How do you know?"

That shrug. "Just do."

They sat in silence for a long while. Then Jez picked up the file folder and waved it. "What did you want me to see this for?"

Walter sighed.

"I didn't know about this," she said, "but I'm not surprised."

He frowned. "This isn't just one or two, uh, *incidents*. How many—*how big is this thing?*"

"I don't know," she said. "Is it any bigger a question than whether there's a heaven and hell?"

"Or whether there's a god?" He cupped his hands together into a big fist, pressed against his mouth.

"Pretty real, ain't it?" She had that conspiratorial smile on her face.

Walter sighed again, resigned. "At least God would know all about love, wouldn't he?"

They sat looking at each other.

Walter finally stood up. "You want coffee?"

Walter and Jez began occasional visits to each other's woodworking shops, chatting informally about their craft but seldom mentioning the alien being or beings that seemed to be observing the humans on Earth.

As with most budding friendships, their conversations gradually became more personal. He talked about his marriage and how he had pretty much shut down emotionally after his wife had left him.

Jez talked about her father, who had mentored her in woodworking and supported her emotionally through a difficult adolescence. After her mother had died, Jez had taken over the household duties for him, and they had spent most of their evenings watching television and talking shop.

"I ain't pretty," she admitted to Walter one evening over drinks. "I didn't think I had any chance to get a husband." She laughed. "Just never gave it much thought."

"Never dated?" Walter was careful to avoid talking about sex with her. She was different from other women he had known, and he wondered if she might be a lesbian.

She chuckled and shrugged. "I asked a fellow out once, when I was in high school, but that didn't go too well, and I never tried it again."

"No friendships?"

Jez closed one eye and looked at him. "I was pretty much a loner. Didn't fit in, didn't really try."

She paused. "Guess Freddy is the only friend I've had in a long time."

That startled Walter. "You call Freddy a friend?"

She frowned. "Yeah," she said. "What else?"

Walter looked away and took a deep breath. "Even if ..."

"You mean because he ain't, ah, *human?*"

Walter laughed. She was so genuine at that point, so *uncluttered,* that he couldn't help but like her. "I'm sorry," he said, "you're right. Even if Freddy isn't like us, you two have some kind of connection. I guess that's friendship—you accept each other as you are."

"Why not?" She seemed perplexed.

"You're right. When I was a kid, I had a dog, and he and I were best friends. We trusted each other more than anybody else in the world. He wasn't just a dog to me. I didn't have any brothers or sisters. Sam was *family.*"

Jez nodded. "Yeah, I get that. Freddy and me are like family, I guess. I don't push on him, and he don't push on me."

"What do you talk about?"

"Sometimes we don't even talk. I might fill him in on stuff he don't understand. He don't know a lot of stuff."

"Like what?"

"Like, stuff about why people act the way they do." She was silent for a moment. "I worry about him sometimes."

"Why is that?"

"He ain't well. I can tell. He sometimes has to stop and catch his breath. Funny, for a guy as young as he is, it's like he's an old man. Sometimes."

"He got folks?" Walter was also beginning to wonder about Freddy. Supposedly he'd been killed by electricity, and then brought back to life. *Like Abigail,* he thought

"Not as far as I know. He never said."

Their conversation trailed off into shop talk, and soon Jez left.

Four

They didn't talk for a couple of weeks, until one evening Jez phoned Walter. "Freddy's gone," she said, her voice catching on the last word.

"He left?"

"No, he just never showed up. We was supposed to install some cabinets over on Wooster Boulevard, but he never showed up."

"You try to call him?"

"No answer."

Walter's mind was running wild. *They've left him and gone to somebody else.* "You want to talk?"

She laughed half-heartedly. "You got any of that good tequila?"

"You betcha. Come on over."

Walter hadn't thought about the aliens in a while. The world hadn't changed. Nothing was reported in the newspapers, and nobody had said anything to remind him. When he did think about *them*, it was from a distance. He lived his life as he had before he found Abigail, worked in his shop and spent a little time with Shep and Charlie, mostly at the bar. They didn't talk about his adventures with the alien, or aliens—he still wasn't sure how to think about the visitors.

Jez was obviously upset when she arrived. Over tequila, she finally said, "I thought he would eventually go someplace else. Maybe he died, after all, and they didn't bring him back. But I thought we'd have a chance to say good bye." Her eyes glistened.

"You've had a lot of loss in your life, and you've had to deal with it alone," Walter said quietly.

"Yeah."

"Do you think they're still around?" He refilled their glasses while he waited for her to answer.

"Don't have a clue."

"You know," he began, "I've wondered if they were getting what they wanted from us. Freddy—or whatever he was—didn't seem to understand us. Oh, he could talk and carry on a conversation, but it was all pretty superficial."

She wiped her cheek with the back of her hand. "I don't understand *you*, sometimes," she said. You're way deeper than I am. All your talk about mirrors and levels of mind or whatever..."

"Sorry. I don't mean to go off on all that. Just how I'm thinking. I get curious. Like I'm curious about *them*. I stopped being scared, I guess. It seemed that Freddy wasn't going to do anything to us. I just wonder what they are, or were after."

She sipped from her glass. "Freddy and I could talk pretty good," she said. "He seemed—I don't know—*real,* somehow. Didn't put on airs. Just said what he thought."

Walter grinned. "Is that what I do? Put on airs?"

She waved a hand. "No, I didn't mean that. Sometimes you're over my head, but I think you're a real person."

"I have feelings," he said. "I don't always show them, but I try to be honest." Walter was aware of feeling the liquor.

She smiled. "They had you pegged right. Maybe they didn't get what they wanted from you, but I did."

"If he comes back—if *they* come back—I'd like to know."

"Okay." She stood up. "I got to move around a little bit. My back gets stiff just sitting."

Walter took a deep breath. "You know," he said, "when I first met you—well, you seem different to me now than you did at first. We could talk about wood working, but I thought that's all."

She smiled at him without speaking.

"There's a lot more to you than I thought. You were able to accept Freddy, or whatever he was, like, at face value. I was always wondering what was behind what he said. You just talked to him like he was an ordinary person asking us questions about regular stuff." Walter looked out the window. "I was, like, wow, what am I into? You know what I mean?"

"A lot of stuff I don't understand," she said. "A lot of what *you* say, I don't understand. Freddy was just a little bit farther out there."

"Yeah, he was."

Jez put her glass down. "I'm feeling steadier," she said. "I just needed to rub up against somebody, I guess." She laughed. "You know what I mean!"

"I do. I'm glad you called me. I said you were in my life now, and I'm comfortable with that. You do good work with your hands, and I admire that."

She picked up her glass and raised it in salute. "Let's do this again."

And she left.

Walter poured himself another tequila. He really did feel comfortable with Jezebel—in spite of her name. He could see why she and Freddy got along, because both of them, on the surface anyway, were *ordinary folks* in the best sense of that term. They didn't pretend to be anything other than themselves.

Freddy, of course, was anything but ordinary. Walter sensed an intellect under that Tennessee drawl, an intellect that had to be far beyond his own. *Far beyond the formerly living Freddy, either,* he thought.

Still, the aliens lacked something that even ordinary humans possess: a gut feeling about relationships. Culture, maybe. The comfort of living with others and sensing a commonality even with strangers. *Isn't that what the word alien means?*

Not all people have that sense of commonality, but when it's missing it usually reflects a life of experiences that hinder its growth. Some people grow up suspicious and fearful of others; some become angry or arrogant to protect themselves from people they see as different from themselves.

He wondered about the differences between the alien-as-Abigail and the alien-as-Freddy. Freddy seemed in control and curious, as though he were an anthropologist studying a distant species. Abigail was fearful, in a situation she didn't understand. In retrospect, she had seemed more human to Walter, struggling to cope with something gone wrong in the system.

They must have a system, too. A plan, for whatever objective. "Here to observe," they said. Maybe a system that was breaking down, and they were—or are— looking for another system that might work for them. Walter got up, a little unsteadily, and went down into his shop. There was nothing he would attempt down there in his present condition. He just wanted to look at his work, at the sturdy chair that awaited varnish, at the little end table that some other workman had made years ago, sure that some unknown person would find it suitable for their purposes, both of them probably now dead. The table still existed.

His fuzzy consciousness pondered, and an odd sense of satisfaction emerged: *They need something that we have, but they think they can get it just by asking questions, seeking data instead of the swirling cocktail of hormones and the layer upon layer of neurons humans have accumulated over eons.*

"Tell me about love," Freddy had asked. Turning toward the stairs, Walter laughed. Rumi must have asked the same thing, but he had that same cluster of cells in his primitive brainstem, and he asked only for the frosting, the end taste of wisdom, not data.

Walter went into his study and withdrew a vinyl record from its sleeve. His hands were now steady as he gently lowered the needle into the groove. *I should have told Freddy to listen to Brahms.*

For the next forty-five minutes, Walter listened. The tequila had worn off by then, leaving him in the thrall of Johannes Brahms, the Nineteenth-Century genius who had all but dominated the Romantic Era of music. *It took him nearly twenty years to create that First Symphony,* Walter thought. *Ha! "Tell me about love." There are millions of words about love, but just listen to* this *and know what it is.*

That night he dreamed about telling—not Freddy, but the intelligence that had inhabited Freddy— about love. "You said you reproduce by 'song'," he told it. "This is *song*—this is how our culture reproduces. Listen to Brahms, or Chopin, or Rachmaninov. This is the juice that flows from mind to mind, that reminds us forever of love and feeling!

He awoke feeling the dried traces of tears on his cheeks. For hours, he lay there thinking of Freddy and Jezebel and Abigail, and of alien beings who knew how to bring the dead back to life but didn't know what human life *means*. He thought about poor Abigail saying, "I wish I were Abigail."

What a mixed up bunch of idiots they are! We humans spend millions of dollars trying to create artificial intelligence in a computer that can think as good as we do, and here these creatures are doing whatever they are doing to learn how to be human— something that is far more than just intelligence.

Maybe time isn't the same to them as it is to us. Maybe to them a thousand years is like a day to us. A day on the moon is twenty-eight of our days. We've evolved over millions of years—could they do it in the blink of an eye?

"Makes one appreciate people more," he said aloud. He sighed, and got out of bed. In his bathrobe, he made a pot of coffee and sat down in his study, listening to music.

The Chopin nocturne brought tears to his eyes.

Five

Walter took in a deep breath of spring air as he set his paper cup on the sidewalk table and sat down next to it. There was little traffic in the street just then, and a number of pedestrians were investigating the shops that had just opened.

"Coffee is good," he said quietly to no one, and propped his iPad up on the table. Skimming the news headlines, he glanced up now and then to take in the scene.

Someone appeared at his side. Before he had time to look up at her, she placed a hand on an adjoining chair and asked, "May I?"

He nodded, and held onto his tablet to make sure it didn't get knocked off the table as she sat. When her face appeared in his field of vision, Walter's heart jumped.

She smiled. "Do I know you?" she asked.

"Uh—of course, Daniele," he stammered. "You're my ex-wife." He couldn't take his eyes off of hers.

There was a twinkle there, the same twinkle he remembered from so many years ago. Her hair was shorter, her clothing less flamboyant. But it was her.

"Is that why I'm here?" She almost laughed, as though she had no idea.

"How are you, Daniele?" He didn't know what to say.

"I'm well," she said gently.

He noticed a faint scar down her cheek. *That was a serious wound,* he thought. Aloud, he said, "It's been six years,"

"Has it?" That little half-laugh again. "I'm afraid I don't remember, but you seem familiar to me."

It took him a long moment to reply. "You have amnesia?"

"I think that's what you call it."

"What happened?" He wondered if it might be connected with the scar on her cheek.

"A long time ago—they've told me it was a couple of years," she said nonchalantly, "They said I fell down some stairs."

His mind whirling, he sipped from his now-cool coffee. "I'm going to have another cup of coffee," he said, getting out of his chair. "Can I get you one?"

"Thank you. Black." Her voice was the same, yet somehow different, as though she had become accustomed to speaking a different language.

As he stood in line to get the coffee, Walter thought about the Daniele he remembered. She now seemed changed—almost more grown up or something. Of course, it had been six years. *We all change over time.*

A little feeling nagged at him.

Walking back outside, he saw her differently, too. The way she held her head, perhaps, was why. *Or an actress, playing the part of Daniele in a stage play.*

But he smiled as he set the two cups down on the table. "You look good, Daniele," he said.

"Thank you." Her smile was almost the same. *Really good actress.*

And then it hit him. He suddenly felt weak. *Abigale. Freddy.* "You're . . ."

"I was called 'Daniele' before."

"Before your amnesia." He still couldn't say it. "Yes."

They sat silently for a few minutes, sipping at their paper cups of coffee in the air of a spring morning. But it was a different spring morning that he felt now, distorted as it was with some kind of reality-unreality shift that he had difficulty navigating through.

"Tell me about Daniele," she said quietly. "I don't remember."

"How did you find me?" he asked.

"I don't know. I felt *pulled here.*"

"Pulled here, from where?"

"Dallas. I was in Dallas."

Walter took a deep breath. "You don't remember me?"

"Tell me," she said.

"We were married," he said, trying to think of how to express what he was feeling.

"Here in this city?"

"Yes. We were married for twelve years. You left me for another man."

"To be with another man?" Her forehead was wrinkled with a struggle to understand. "Why?"

"I guess you got tired of me." Walter felt caught up in an old, not completely forgotten state of mind. Of bewilderment, of loss, of anger. "I felt like you had just turned me off—turned a switch. When you said good bye, you didn't even look me in the eye."

She was looking into his eyes now, with something like sadness, but a lack of understanding. "Why would I have done that?"

He thought of Abigale that night, struggling to understand him in the most obvious situations. Memories flooded his mind with the feeling of that woman suddenly straddling him in her apartment, following some ancient impulse that had little to do with him as a person—a human being—yet seeming skilled at the task at hand.

"You would never have done that," he said, and then suddenly aware of how little that would mean to her.

"Oh, that. I should have been embarrassed, shouldn't I?" She laughed.

The full force of it hit him. "You remember that." Walter nodded. "You're one of them."

She smiled. "You are still on guard."

He sighed deeply, and leaned back in his chair, as though to put this woman—this creature—into perspective. "You look like my wife—my former wife—and yet you are not her, are you?"

"Who am I?" she asked, sounding innocent.

"Not who," he answered, "What are you?"

"You said, one time, that you still loved me, after all those years."

He frowned, trying to remember. "I told that to Freddie, about my ex-wife."

Walter was sweating now. His heart was pounding. He knew what was going on, and yet he didn't. They were playing a game, and it seemed that she had no more idea of the game than he did. "You're here to observe, aren't you?"

She frowned. "Yes," she said finally. "You know that?"

"Why come to me?"

"I don't know." She lowered her head and looked into the small opening in the lid of her coffee, as though there might be an answer there among the brown bubbles turning cold. "I have a longing," she said slowly, and then looked up at him. "This human I inhabit—this former human—gives me feelings, impulses, half-memories . . . many of which are about you, now I recognize." She smiled. "When I first found you here just now, it was like I had been carried along in a breeze for a long time, and suddenly it became a solid thing, a thread, attached to you."

Walter was no longer sweating. In a way, he felt strong in this situation. This creature knew less about him than he did about her—or them.

"You don't understand emotional relationships, do you?" he asked, trying not to challenge her.

"You loved her—this Daniele—didn't you?" She was meeting his gaze.

"Yes." He paused. "She's dead, isn't she?" He felt a slight tug in his midsection as he said it.

Daniele nodded.

"How much of her is still alive in you?"

"Most of her body," she said, pinching her arm. "She was healthy and strong. Her mind is almost infinitely complex. We're trying to make connections."

He smiled wryly. "I worked hard to try to understand her mind. In the end, I was unsuccessful."

"She broke off your relationship, you said."

He shrugged. "I guess she fell for another man."

"I thought humans were generally monogamous."

Walter had to smile. "So did I."

"You are very kind," she said.

Walter was caught by her words. "You—she—Abigale—said that, *just that way*, in her apartment."

Daniele smiled. "Did I?"

"Yes."

"What did it mean to you?" Her voice was honey.

Walter lowered his gaze to his hands. Then he looked up into her eyes. "I guess it took me by surprise," he said. "Abigail was so distant before that, as though she didn't see me at all and was only concerned by her feeling abandoned by the others. She was reaching out to me."

Daniele was silent for a moment, then: "I was new then. I didn't know what to expect."

He smiled. "You took a risk."

She cocked her head. "Yes, I did, didn't I? I had a sudden *feeling* about you." She smiled, and held her arms wide. "It was like a song, brewing somewhere. In you. In you and me. Something special."

He smiled, but said nothing, thinking. Then, "A song."

She nodded. "Does that make sense to you? I'm not sure I understand it."

Walter's hands were shaking.

"What is that?" she asked, indicating his hands.

"He sighed. "I don't' know. Something that comes from stress or uncertainty. An unintentional reflex."

"What does it tell you?"

"Christ, you sound like a therapist! I don't know. Let's see, I'm tense from this conversation because I don't know where it's heading."

"I'm only here to observe." She said it with a straight face, but her eyes were twinkling.

He managed a smile. "Unbelievable. You tell me that Daniele is dead, and yet there's something of her in you, in her body. In one way, it's horrible, but in another way I want to grasp what's left of her."

"I'm sorry." Her face was sad.

He looked up, surprised. "Where does that come from?"

Her eyebrows raised, echoing his question.

"I don't' know what you feel!" he exclaimed. "All of the conversations I've had with you—with Abigail, with Freddy—have left me with the understanding that you cannot grasp emotions like humans do. Do you know what that feels like, to be sorry?"

She looked at him for a long time. Finally, she said, "Walter, we are learning. Yes, I feel—here—" She pointed to her chest. "I don't' know what it is yet. It's something that she felt."

Walter slumped in the chair. "I wonder," he said quietly, "if she felt sorry about us."

Daniele frowned thoughtfully. "I don't know," the alien said.

"You don't know grief," Walter said, and sighed.

"I'm feeling something here," she said, pointing again at her chest, "that comes from you." She took his hand and placed it on her breast. "Is that grief?"

Walter folded his arms on the table and put his head down and began to sob. He felt a hand on his shoulder.

"I'm sorry," she said softly.

Suddenly he needed her to be Daniele. Looking up into her face, barely registering the scar there, he saw the woman he had loved for twelve years—no, *eighteen years.*

A tear welled up in one of her eyes and slid down her cheek. Suddenly she stood back, a strange look on her face. "I have to go," she said, turning away.

"Wait!" he shouted to her. "Where are you going?"

"I'll find you again, Walter."

The memory of his hand, guided by hers, on her breast stayed with him for days. How much of Daniele remained in that body? In that mind?

He finally phoned Jez. "Thought you might be interested," he said. "They are back."

Jez waited. Then she asked, "Freddie?"

"No." Walter choked up and had a hard time speaking. "My ex-wife, Daniele."

"I don't get it."

"Only it's not her."

"You think . . . "

"I *know.*" Walter took a deep breath. "She just came up to me, in front of the Coffee Bean on Front Street. She said she couldn't remember who I was, but she came right up to *me.*"

"Your ex-wife." Jez didn't have many words.

"She admitted who she—what she was. She's the same as Freddie, the same as Abigail."

"Holy smokes." Jez paused. "She say what happened to your ex?"

Walter's voice caught. "She fell down some stairs."

Jez was quiet for a moment. "How you doin', Friend? You said you still loved her."

Walter took a moment to reply. "Lemme call you back," he said.

"Gotcha." Jez hung up.

The next day was Sunday, and Walter sat with a bottle of vodka and listened to Sibelius's Fifth. In the early evening, his phone rang. It was Daniele's phone calling. His heart pounding, he answered. "You still have her phone," he said.

"Your number is still in it," she replied.

His mind seemed scrambled. "Still," was all he could say.

"Can we talk?" It was undoubtedly Daniele's voice.

"You know where I live?"

"Yes."

Walter kept losing his place. *How could she know where I live?*

"Okay," he said finally. "Now?"

"Yes."

The doorbell sounded within minutes, startling him. *She must have been out front when she called.*

Her short hair and the scar on her cheek took him aback for a moment. "I don't know what to say," he said. He gestured toward a chair.

Daniele smiled, and Walter felt like crying.

"I'm sorry," she said. "This must be hard for you."

He nearly shouted, *"How would you know?"* But he swallowed, took a deep breath, and said, "I haven't seen her in a long time."

"No."

"Why?" he started, then took another deep breath, "why do you have to look like her?"

"I'm here to observe," she said simply.

"Goddamn it! What's that mean?"

She smiled again, and waited until his breathing quieted. "You and Daniele had a close relationship."

"Yes," he said, his voice still high and strained. "We did have—and then she left!"

Daniele started to put a hand on his, but stopped. "Two days ago, when we first met," she said, "I was picking up things from you, and from her—I think—that I needed to study."

Walter stood and got the vodka bottle from the table, then collected two glasses from the breakfront. Setting them on the coffee table, he said, "I don't know about you, but I need this."

She smiled again. "Abigail drank vodka, didn't she?"

Quietly, "My god," was all he could say. He poured the liquor into both glasses. "You've come a long way from Abigail."

Momentarily, she seemed perplexed.

Downing the vodka in a single gulp, he set the glass down and for the first time, he smiled.

Daniele's brow smoothed out again. "You told Freddie—" and she paused, "that you still loved Daniele. What does that mean to you?"

The heat in his throat from the drink was beginning to wane, yielding to a warmth that flooded his consciousness. "I still love you, Daniele," he said quietly. "For a while I hated you, too."

She smiled. "That's why I come to you as her."

"To confuse me?"

"No," she said, "no. Just the opposite."

Neither of them spoke for a long time.

Then Daniele said, "I didn't stop loving you, Walter. I just couldn't face you."

"What was it—an airline pilot?"

"I think so," she said. "From what I can gather from her memories—and the feelings connected with them—Daniele never felt about him the way she felt about you."

"Then why did she leave?" Walter was trying hard to control his voice.

"I wonder that, too."

He slumped. "I guess I wasn't very exciting."

"Exciting? What does that mean?"

He had to smile. "One minute I'm looking at Daniele, and then I'm hearing somebody who never knew Daniele."

"Tell me about *exciting*." She spoke the word as if it were in Hungarian or something.

"Exciting is arousing, usually sexually. Something, or someone, who is exciting stimulates you, leaves you a little breathless, uncertain but—but *aroused* in some way."

"Abigail was aroused by you." She seemed somehow satisfied with the thought.

Walter's face colored slightly, but he grinned. "That's the idea," he said.

"Abigail found you exciting." She smiled back.

Walter poured another drink. Daniele watched him, then picked up her own glass and drank.

"I'm feeling something," she said after a moment. "Warm." She pointed to her throat.

"Alcohol does that," he said, still smiling. "Give it another minute and you'll feel something else."

Her eyebrows rose just a trifle.

"It relaxes you," he said. "Makes you loose."

"Loose. Not the same as excited?"

"No. But . . ." He took a moment to breathe deeply and let it out. "It's like you don't care so much about how other people see you."

Daniele shook her head.

"It's like," and he smiled, "you are more aware of what's going on in your own mind, er, body."

"Hormones."

It was his turn to feel confused. "Where did you hear about hormones?"

"I think you used the term explaining to Freddie."

He laughed out loud. "Oh, my god!"

Daniele smiled sweetly and looked down at her hands.

"Okay," he said, "right now, are you Daniele, or . . ."

One beautiful eyebrow went up an eighth of an inch. After a moment, she said, "I see what you mean."

"You're feeling it?"

"Hormones. Yes. And alcohol."

Walter slumped back. His face was sad.

She took a deep breath and let it out slowly. "I'm sorry, Walter, that you lost her."

His voice was husky with emotion. "It's like watching an old home movie of someone who has died."

"I suspect," she said, "that it's more than that. A home movie wouldn't be able to converse with you."

"No."

"But this is very important for me—for us."

Just for a second, Walter could see behind the Daniele façade. There was *something* there, something that was not Daniele. "You are . . ."

She nodded, her face showing sadness, a different sadness than his sorrow of a moment before. "I feel . . ."

"Compassion," he said, watching her eyes. "Feeling other people's emotions."

"Yes."

She looked at him silently for a long time. Then she reached across the coffee table and took his hand. Very softly, she asked, "Walter, do you want to make love to Daniele, one last time?"

Startled, he drew back.

"Just her. Nobody else. Nothing else. Just you and Daniele."

Daniele sat and waited, her eyes never leaving his.

Walter breathed deeply several times. This was Daniele, the woman he had loved for as long as he could remember, facing him, offering herself to him. And it wasn't. It was an alien being in her skin, with her words, her expression, her love. No.

"No," he said. "Thank you. No. My body—my *soul*, it feels like—wants very much to feel Daniele against me again. But you're not Daniele, and I couldn't make love to you. I've passed up the chance for sex with several women since Daniele left, because *they weren't her*. What happened between Abigale and me was just sex, and it felt good for a few minutes, but then it felt awful. I've been ashamed ever since."

Daniele's face changed subtly, but she continued to hold his gaze.

"I wasn't a very good person that night," he said. "I should have left her at the emergency room, let the professionals take care of her. I should never have drunk that vodka. I was irresponsible. Maybe if we hadn't had sex I could have faced the young man— Michael—and helped him take care of her. But my shame made me have to escape."

"You kept saying that you didn't know what to do," the alien said quietly.

He shrugged. "I was completely dumbfounded."

"What does that have to do with Daniele?" the alien asked. "You said you still love her."

"I love her memory. You look like her, but you're not her." He burst into tears and turned away. "Go away!"

As he buried his face in a pillow, he heard her get up quietly and go out the door.

After a long time, he sat up and wiped his face, looking across the room at where she had sat. It was as if her ghost still sat there. He shook off the impression.

Walter became aware of something else, a thought that gradually put itself together in his mind. It seemed the alien had learned something, It was *feeling something* for Walter. Maybe it was compassion. In his first conversations with it as Freddy, it wanted to know about sex and procreation, and then it wanted to know about love. Now, it seemed, there was something more.

Compassion is a kind of love, an undemanding wish to give, to help. In the beginning of a relationship, sex is a motivator to tighten the bond, but the bond is the thing. Like he tried to tell Freddy, there's a part of a relationship that gives and a part that takes. For a while, it's important that each one gives and takes more or less equally. Maybe he hadn't ever grown past the taking part with Daniele—that's why he suffered so much, and for so long.

When he was offered the gift—what the alien thought was what he wanted—his body responded almost automatically. It meant little to the alien.

Or maybe it did. Maybe, in Daniele's body, it was more than a gift. Maybe at that moment it was more than generosity. Maybe Walter had become more than just useful to its purposes. Perhaps the alien *felt what Walter was feeling*, and like a human, was responding with what it thought he needed.

Walter still struggled to keep them separate. Part of him still clung to Daniele, or the thought of Daniele, like clutching an old photograph. Daniele, animated by the alien, was not Daniele.

He put the vodka and the glasses away, and went downstairs to his shop. The odors of varnish and fresh cut wood returned him to himself, at least for now. Daniele was dead, and now he might be able to look to his future, instead of his past.

Six

(Twenty Years On . . .)

The faint notes of the nocturne carried through the incessant throb of the engines as Walter picked up the two brandies from the counter and turned toward the music. Each perfect note owned the ear for an instant—a warm raindrop touching an upturned face, recognizable in that instant and then immediately blending with a thousand others caressing the skin—each note forever tucked into memory creating with its mates a feeling of *rightness.* "She does love Chopin," he said quietly to himself.

The soft light in the lounge wrapped around him, and he found an empty seat, setting the two glasses on the little table in front of him. He caught her eye and was rewarded with a flick of smile. The nocturne continued.

This cruise was his reward to himself for decades of office boredom, but he forgot the open sea outside the walls of the lounge, instead sinking every day into luxurious upholstery to listen to her play the piano.

Several pairs of hands clapped softly when she finished the piece; then she placed her own hands into her lap for a moment. She nodded and smiled shyly in acknowledgment.

He picked up one of the glasses to salute her, and he patted the seat next to him.

She silently obeyed his gesture, gliding over to him.

"Your playing makes me want to live forever," he said.

"Thank you." She picked up one of the glasses and sipped.

"Will you have dinner with me later?" He asked.

She nodded, holding his eye.

Walter was still basking in his retirement. At first, he had spent his days in his shop, sanding smooth curves of furniture. Then he went away on the Caribbean cruise that he had promised himself for years. He hadn't been prepared for the loneliness of watching a thousand other people laughing, talking and playing together. He was used to being alone, but always in the privacy of his cubicle or the comfort of his little woodworking shop. In the midst of crowded gaiety he missed intimacy.

Until Clara.

Their quiet conversations over dinner led eventually to soft nights in his room.

They sat under an umbrella, eating lunch. "I want to find another place to live," he told her. "Some place with a view, but still having a wood shop."

"You want water or mountains?" Clara had been holding his hand, and now squeezed it.

"Both would be great. Mostly I want some visual stimulation."

"Music?"

"Of course," he said. "A big room, a big sound system." He paused. "Maybe a piano."

Her eyebrows went up. "Do you play?"

He grinned and shook his head. "Maybe I'll learn."

"Sounds awesome."

He took her hand in both of his. "How would you like to help me find a place?"

Clara looked down. "I don't know," she said softly.

"I'm sorry." He chuckled. "I'm getting ahead of us, aren't I?"

"You like my playing," she said, her voice becoming sad. "We have different lives."

Still holding her hand, he said, "I've just begun a new life. I can live anywhere. I would like very much if we could at least see each other once in a while."

"But you don't know anything about me, besides my piano playing." She withdrew her hand.

"I know more than you think."

She looked into his eyes. "Do you?"

"Yes."

She continued to hold his gaze for a long time.

"Am I too needy?" He asked finally.

Dropping her eyes, she said, "I don't understand a lot about life. I've been pretty sheltered."

"Where's your family?"

She stood. "I have to get back to my piano."

They walked together back to the lounge. The other occupants had left.

Standing beside the piano, she looked up at him, "Both of my parents died," she said. "I don't know if I have any other family. I just play music."

He started to put an arm around her shoulders, then thought better of it. "You play music on cruise ships. That's all?"

She sat down at the piano and smiled. "Not much of a life, is it?"

He sighed. "I thought *my* life was pretty empty."

Turning toward him, she said, "But you seem so—so, *cosmopolitan.*" And she laughed.

Another couple entered the lounge. They looked around. "I thought somebody would be playing the piano here," one said.

Clara stood up. "That's me," she said. "I was just taking a break."

"Classical, right?"

Clara opened the piano. "Do you like Schumann?"

The woman laughed. "I don't know much about music. I think so."

Clara began to play.

The couple clapped when she finished the piece. "That's Robert Schumann?" the woman asked.

Clara smiled. "Clara Schumann."

The man looked at the placard standing next to the piano. "Clara Schumann—that's you?"

Clara laughed. "No. I just happen to have the same name."

"Relative?"

She smiled. "Only by her music."

"Robert and Clara were husband and wife," Walter said. "A lot of people think she was the greater of the two."

Clara flashed him a smile. "My parents thought I should have a famous name, and they loved the Schumanns' works."

"That would be a lot to live up to," the man said.

She turned the smile on him. "Sometimes it is." And then she began another piece without opening the sheet music in front of her.

The ship was nearing its home port, and passengers were setting their luggage out in the hallways.

Walter and Clara sat at the bar, having "one last drink."

"I'm not ready to say goodbye," he said, looking into her eyes.

Clara laughed. "The next cruise leaves on Thursday," she said.

"Why don't you get off with me? We'll go house hunting."

She laughed again, but looked down at her hands. "Walter, . . ." she began, and looked up at him.

"I know," he said. "You don't have any reason to trust me."

"Yes I do."

"Can you take some time off this job, and we'll just travel a little bit together. And just maybe in the process find me a new home."

"I have a contract," she said, "but I suppose they can always find another musician."

"Then what?"

"I don't' know." She looked at him, tears welling up in her eyes. "I DON'T KNOW!"

Surprised, he put his hand on hers. "Hey," he said, "I get it. You're just not ready." He sighed deeply. "It's been so long since I have felt this way about anyone. I just don't want to lose you!"

She looked out of the large window near them. The coast was visible ahead. People were on deck, hurrying back and forth.

She turned back to face him. "All right," she said. "I have to tell my boss, and I have to pack my things."

Walter's heart leaped in his chest. "Okay, come on. I'll help you."

They stood and embraced, then hurried toward her room. At the door, she inserted her key in the lock and looked up at him. "You're very kind," she said, then went through the door.

Walter felt the hairs on the back of his neck move. Then he followed her in.

A little while later, they went down the gangway together, holding hands and grinning at each other.

When they had located their luggage on the dock, he said, "You stand guard here, and I'll take the shuttle to the parking lot. I'll be back in a few minutes."

She was still standing by the luggage when he pulled up with his car.

He stood on the veranda with a beer in his hand, looking out over the lake to the mountains beyond. A gentle breeze came in off the water, and he wondered if one of those little float planes could land and take off there. *Could save a couple of hour's drive if we had one,* he thought.

Chopin was drifting out from the living room, where Clara was practicing. He loved the music in the house, and he loved the way she played with such feeling.

Clara had little knowledge or interest in cooking, so Walter had taken charge of their meals. She was quite fastidious about the way their home looked, however, bringing in flowers and hanging new pictures on the walls occasionally. He spent time in his wood working shop while she practiced on the piano. The sound of the piano, when it was not drowned out by the machinery in his shop, gave Walter a lot of pleasure.

He'd bought the piano for her even before they moved into the house. "I want to learn to play, too," he had said, "but only if you have the patience."

She had smiled and kissed him. "I'd love to."

Occasionally, they invited friends in to listen to her play, and she enjoyed "performing," as she called it.

Living in such a rural area, they didn't have many neighbors, but had met most of them at the local pub that was the only business at the local crossroads. It was a congenial group, mostly professionals, and the juke box in the pub even played some popular classical music.

"I met Clara on an ocean cruise," he told the group once, "shortly after I retired, almost fifteen years ago. She was playing in one of those quiet little lounges on the ship that had a piano and a group of easy chairs. She played mostly Chopin and Schumann—both Robert's and Clara's."

He looked at Clara. "When I asked her name during a pause in her playing, she laughed and said that her parents had loved the original Clara Schumann's music so much they named their daughter after that famous composer."

"It just happened," Clara told them, "that I took to the piano from an early age. "Maybe it was their encouragement, as well as my name that drew me to the piano."

One of the wives looked at Walter. "You went on a cruise by yourself?" she asked.

"The cruise was my reward to myself for thirty years of dull office work," he responded, repeating what he'd told many others. "Some friends tried to get me to take a lady along with me, but female companionship always seemed to take more effort than it was worth."

"And then you met Clara." Everybody laughed.

"My first marriage was a long time before," he said. "I never thought I'd ever do that again."

He and Clara held each other's eyes for a long time, until somebody broke the spell by spilling their drink.

"Where are you from, originally?" someone asked Clara.

"I grew up in Vienna," she said.

"But you don't have any accent at all, that I can hear."

Clara blushed slightly. "I think I've forgotten all of my original language." She smiled shyly. "I've been an American almost as long as I can remember."

"You know, I never thought of that," Walter said. He looked at Clara. "You could pass for a Midwesterner any day of the week"

Another person asked, "Where did you live before you joined the cruise line and traveled the world?"

Clara paused and looked down at her hands. "Columbus, I think," she said.

"Columbus, Ohio, right? Couldn't be Columbus Georgia with that accent!" Everybody laughed.

Clara glanced nervously at Walter, then got up and went to the juke box. She played an old recording by José Iturbi, "Clair de Lune."

"Yes. Thank you," said Clara to her phone as Walter came up the stairs from his wood shop.

When she disconnected, Walter asked, "What was that about?"

She smiled. "I'm going on another cruise. Do you want to come?"

"What?"

"My old boss from the cruise line just called and asked if I could fill in for the pianist he had scheduled on a cruise next week but they came down with the flu."

Walter frowned, and looked at the calendar on his phone. "I have a hematologist appointment on Wednesday," he said.

"Do you mind if I go without you?" Clara put a hand on his arm.

He grinned. "As if I could stop you."

"No, really, Walter," she said. "I want to play again, but not if you're against it. It's only a week."

"Where's the cruise?"

"It leaves from Houston on Saturday and goes down to Belize and back."

"Well, go, of course."

She embraced him. "I'll miss you, you know." Leaning her head back so that she could see his face, she said, "I remember how nice it was that time, to see you sitting there every day while I played."

A s she sat in the dim lounge at the piano, Clara thought about the first time she had seen Walter. There was something about him that she had immediately felt drawn to.

Three times a day, she played for an hour all of her favorite pieces from Chopin and the two Schumanns. Once, someone asked her to play a Liszt etude. She responded, "I'm sorry, I don't play Liszt. He just doesn't fit my style."

Another woman in the lounge spoke up: "The other Clara Schumann wouldn't play him, either."

Clara smiled. "Maybe it's a family trait," she said.

The woman approached the piano. "I remember you," she said. "You used to be a concert pianist, a long time ago, weren't you?"

"When I was young," Clara answered, and began to play.

After the piece, the woman spoke again. "I heard that you had been killed in an automobile accident. Was that not you?"

Clara laughed. "Obviously, I didn't die, did I? I was badly injured, and I had to retire from the concert circuit."

"You were good, though. I still have a recording you made with the Rochester Orchestra."

"That was a long time ago," Clara said.

The woman smiled. "I'm glad you're still playing."

"Thank you."

At Clara's last scheduled appearance in the lounge before their return to Houston, the woman appeared briefly and left her a generous tip.

On the airplane back home, she thought about those years after the accident and how difficult it had been to learn to play all over again. About the accident itself, she had no memory. Her hands, she found, remembered.

Her reunion with Walter gave her profound joy.

Walter was not well. The hematologist told him that his bone marrow was not replenishing his blood well enough, and they scheduled a series of transfusions.

Clara learned to cook and help him bathe, and the two of them grew even closer as time went on. When he felt well enough to work in his wood shop, he managed to finish a cherry desk chair that he had begun years before but had set aside in order to make other furniture for their home.

After some months, it was apparent to both of them that Walter's time was near. Clara sat by his bedside every day, or went into the living room to play for him.

"Clara," he said quietly one day, "promise me something?"

"Of course, my love."

"Don't let them take me."

She looked at him quickly. "What do you mean?"

"You know," he said, managing a weak smile.

Clara burst into tears, and buried her face in the pillow next to him. He reached up and patted her shoulder.

"How long have you known?" she asked softly.

"Long time," he answered. "It was years after we got together, and there were little clues, every once in a while." He looked into her eyes. "Once—I don't remember when—you said something to me, 'You are very kind,' and I flashed on those words, spoken in that exact way, from before we knew each other. Do you remember?"

"Of course."

"You have learned a lot about being human," he said. "When I began to realize who you were, I didn't want to admit it to myself. I didn't want to admit it to you. By that time I loved you too much. If it was all a sham, I was willing to live the sham with you."

She sat up and took his hand in hers. "My love was—my love is—not a sham," she said. "You have taught me so much about what it is to be human."

"Even before we met, you had learned a lot," he said. "I didn't guess, for a long time. By the time I felt sure, it was okay. I still loved you, whatever that means."

"Just now you asked me to promise you."

"Yes. I've had a good life. I can't imagine living without you—my Clara. You don't need my body."

"Clara can't imagine living without you, either," the alien said, holding his gaze.

He looked out the window. "I'm impressed," he said, his voice husky, "how you were able to pick up her piano talent. You play so wonderfully," and he looked back into her eyes, "so full of feeling."

"We talked, you and I, a long time ago, about our songs." She stroked his forehead gently.

"I remember," he said, smiling.

"You are dying soon."

"Yes."

"So will Clara." She held his gaze. "She will lie down with you and she will leave with you."

"I love you," he managed to say, and closed his eyes.

Clara Schumann lay down beside him.

The song remained.

Daniele

One

She heard voices behind her, and moved to the side to let a woman and a small girl pass by. The woman turned and smiled at her. The girl said "Scuse us please."

Daniele smiled back, and watched the couple stroll out on the breakwater.

I wonder what she meant by that, thought Daniele. *She seemed to be apologizing. For what? Perhaps for moving through Daniele's space? People sometimes surround themselves with an area that they claim as if their self extends some distance out from their skins. Most people don't like to be touched by strangers. How far does Daniele's space extend?*

Daniele spent a lot of time analyzing her experiences with people. The remark by a child suggested a social sensitivity that Daniele had not noticed before. She stored the bit of knowledge to be thought more about later, and turned her attention to her present environment.

The afternoon air was thick over Lake Michigan. On the western horizon, the sun gradually merged into a line of blue-gray clouds that looked like an opposite shoreline but wasn't.

Daniele removed her sunglasses and basked in the orange glow. People strolled along the breakwater and occasional boats moved slowly through the channel. The Beaver Island ferry had just passed under the drawbridge, dwarfing the pleasure craft that moved out of its way. A slight breeze off the lake felt cool on her bare legs.

She had come to enjoy this place, this little tourist town that in warm weather teamed with pedestrians and automobiles, and seemed almost deserted when snow covered everything. When she had arrived here several years before, the first light snows of the season had barely covered the still-green grass. That first winter was horrible for her, keeping her indoors most of the time, and isolated.

But even then, there was a charm to the place. The few year-round residents were friendlier toward each other. She found that they were more open with her when she asked questions. "You're not from around here, are you?" some asked. But they patiently described whatever she inquired about, a foreigner welcomed when tourists were few.

She met Timmy as she bought groceries at Oleson's one winter. "Why aren't you away at school?" she asked him as he bagged her groceries.

"Ran out of money," he said. "I was up in Marquette, but my dad stopped supporting me." He laughed. "Seemed to think I was enjoying it too much."

She ran into him again on Main Street the following week, in late afternoon after the winter sun had long disappeared, recognizing him in the light of a streetlamp. They both stopped.

She spoke first: "What do you do on these dark, cold days—besides bagging people's groceries?"

He shrugged. "Never got into snowmobiling," he said. "I sit home at my computer a lot, trading barbs with people on Twitter."

"I'm here to observe," she said. "Would you spend some time with me and let me probe your mind?"

He looked at her quizzically. "You a psychologist?"

"No, why?"

"I had a class in psych last year. Interesting." He grinned at her. "I can't get into that Freudian stuff, but I liked the part about psycho-neurology," and he stumbled over the word, "or is it neuro-psychology? Figuring out how all that stuff is connected in the brain."

She smiled. "Me, too."

"How come you're around here in the winter? All the other tourists leave for the south."

"It's quiet here. I'm studying." She pulled her fur collar tighter against a sudden cold wind.

"What are you studying? You said you're not a psychologist."

She grinned, peering out at him from inside her hood. "I'm studying people. Is that psychology?"

"You writing a book?"

"Not exactly," she said, stamping her feet against the cold. "Could we go inside someplace to talk?"

He looked around. "Simonsen's is right over there. They're still open."

"Wonderful."

They trudged through the snow to the café. Inside, they were the only customers. They selected a table away from the door and sat down.

"Coffee?" he asked, and she nodded, slowly undoing her parka.

When the proprietor brought their coffee, he set a small dish down with two scones, as well. "On the house," he said.

"Thank you," she said, smiling at him.

They sipped their coffee for a moment without speaking. Then Tim said, "You said you *weren't exactly* writing a book. What's that mean?"

She grinned, and put out her hand. "I'm Daniele," she said.

"Tim," he said, holding her hand for a moment. "What's that mean?"

"You are persistent, aren't you?"

"Well?"

Daniele laughed. "You're very curious about me," she said, "I'm curious about people in general."

He frowned and smiled at the same time.

She broke a corner off one of the scones and nibbled on it. "How old are you, Tim?"

Grinning, he said, "Old enough."

"Old enough. I don't know what that means." She glanced at the proprietor, who was watching them from behind the counter.

"I'm twenty-two."

"So young!"

"You're laughing at me."

"I'm not!"

"Okay," he said, grinning, "how old are you?"

She stopped for a moment, thinking.

Tim laughed. "See? That's embarrassing, isn't it?"

"No," she said. "I can't really remember. About forty, I think."

He looked at her, surprised. "You can't remember how old you are?"

"I uh, had amnesia, and I haven't gotten all of my life back yet."

"Oh," he said, "that why you're studying psychology?"

"Psychology?"

"Isn't that—no, you said you were studying *people*."

Daniele laughed. "I suppose you have to start with your own mind, don't you—if you want to study people."

He chuckled and shook his head. "You're something else."

Something flickered across her face that he didn't recognize. "What do you mean?" she asked.

He feigned patience. "Saying 'you're something else' just means you're different somehow."

"Not what you expected."

"Exactly."

They sat for a few minutes, sipping coffee and eating the scones.

"I want—" she began, "I want to know how people think and feel. I'm just studying."

Still grinning, he said, "Never heard of anybody doing that. It's a little weird, if you don't mind my saying it."

"I told you that I had amnesia, and I don't have all my life back yet." She sipped her coffee, watching him. "So I'm studying."

He nodded. "Okay, that makes sense. What don't you remember—besides your age?"

"I have only faint memories of my life before about ten years ago. I get feelings, sometimes, that must have come from earlier things because they aren't connected with what I do remember."

"So you don't know who your mother and your father are—or were."

"No."

"Brothers or sisters?"

"No."

He leaned back in the chair. "That's weird. It's like you were just born—what'd you say, ten years ago?"

"That's an interesting way to put it."

Tim leaned forward and rested his elbows on the table. "So, maybe you're somebody's wife, even." He pointed at her hand. "You're not wearing a ring."

She shrugged. "I had a glimpse, a few years ago, of someone who might have been in my life before, but I'm not sure."

He grinned. "You sure are a mystery woman!"

Daniele looked thoughtful. After a moment she said, "Yes."

He touched the scar on her cheek. "How'd you get that? Or shouldn't I ask?"

"They told me I had fallen down some stairs."

"That when you got amnesia?"

"I think so." She touched her cheek where his fingers had been.

"Wow," he said softly. "I'm sorry."

She smiled. "Thank you."

"It's not—" he said, studying the scar. "It's not like it's disfiguring or anything. It's just interesting."

She stood up and went to the counter, where the proprietor had been pretending not to listen. Taking a bill from her purse, she handed it to him.

The man pressed keys on the cash register. "Coffee, a dollar fifty—three eighteen, altogether."

"Thank you for the scones."

"My pleasure. Come in again."

Outside on the dark, wind-blown sidewalk, she turned to Tim, "I'm on my way to the grocery store—where you work."

"I was just off my shift, but if you want some help carrying groceries home, ..."

She looked up the street, then turned her head, peering at him past the fur trim of her hood. "That would be lovely," she said.

Later, each carrying an arm full of groceries, they turned onto a walk that led to an exterior stairway on the side of a large older house.

"I get lots of exercise getting to my home," she said. "I'm glad the owner clears the steps."

They mounted the stairway to a door on the second floor, where she handed him her grocery bag before fishing keys from her purse.

Inside, the room was rather dark but warm. She took the bags from him and set them on a table. "This is where I live."

"Feels good in here," he said, looking around.

"Thank you for your help." She removed her parka and hung it on a peg. "Can I fix you something? Coffee, vodka? I don't have any beer."

"Vodka." He took off his coat. "I like vodka, just ice."

"On the rocks," she said hesitantly. "That's what it's called?"

He looked at her, one eyebrow lifted a little. "You don't know that?"

Pouring their drinks, she laughed. "I think I remember that, but I'm not sure about a lot of things."

She took her glass and sat on a small sofa. "I don't have many chairs."

He sat beside her and awkwardly stretched his legs out. Lifting his glass, he said, "Here's to winter in Charlevoix."

"That restaurant down on Main Street by the canal has a wonderful fireplace," she said, sipping her drink. When it's cold outside, it feels so good to go in there and just sit near the fire."

"Yeah, Weathervane."

After a few moments, he looked at her and asked, "You have folks around here?"

"No," she said, "I came up here about two years ago, with a man I knew in Detroit." She glanced at him and laughed. "We had a misunderstanding, and he went back without me."

"Wow."

"It was in the beginning of winter. It was awful, that winter."

"You didn't live in the north, before?"

"No." She smiled. "You've probably lived here all your life."

"My folks are from Kalkaska. When I had to drop out of NMU, I came here. I like the water—at least in the summer. I worked on the ferry for a while."

They sat in silence for a few minutes, sipping their drinks. Then he turned toward her. "You're very pretty," he said.

She smiled, glancing quickly at him. "Would you like to make love with me?"

"Sure." But he didn't put his glass down.

"Let's finish our drinks first," she said. "It makes it easier."

He looked at her without speaking, and then took another sip from his drink, looking straight ahead. She noticed that his ears had become pink.

After a few minutes of silence, Daniele stood up and reached her hand toward him. He took her hand and allowed her to lead him toward a bed that almost filled a small alcove. They put their glasses on the table as they passed.

"You seem—shy," she said.

He didn't answer.

They sat on the edge of the bed. Tim looked quickly at her, then down at his clasped hands. Finally, he said, "I've never done this before."

"You've watched it on television and movies, I'm sure," she said. "Is it that hard for you?"

He laughed, and his face colored noticeably. "I don't know. Yeah, I don't know. I knew a girl once, in school, and she wanted to do it but I guess she got tired of waiting." He looked at her, his face contorted. "I don't even know how to start."

"It's all right. I was just like you at one time." She began unbuttoning her blouse.

Later, Daniele lay quietly watching patterns of light playing across the ceiling. Tim was asleep beside her. Looking over at him, she smiled. He was different, this boy, from the other men she had known. He'd been careful with her, as though he was afraid of hurting her, but once inside her he had orgasmed almost immediately. She didn't mind when he rolled over and dropped off to sleep; she was used to men doing that.

Ever since *the fall*—that's how she thought of it to herself—she had been exploring this world and how it affected her. Her body presented such a myriad of feelings, some seemingly connected to vague memories from before, but others like flashes of colored lights without sources, mysteriously engulfing her, then gradually fading away. She eventually decided that they resulted from some unknown hormonal activities. *Studying* became her life.

Men, in particular, fascinated her. She was curious about other women, assuming that many of her experiences were common to them, but she was drawn to men. Getting them to pay attention to her was seldom a problem; getting them to tell her what they were experiencing was almost always difficult.

After the first years, she developed a quick sense of what behavior to expect from a man she had just met. Nearly all were eager for sex. A few seemed inexplicably to dislike her even before talking with her, as though she showed some trait that branded her an enemy, or something. Occasionally, she'd met a man who seemed friendly but kept at a distance—"married", she learned, committed to another woman and cautious with her.

So many kinds of people! Each one different not only in appearance but in temperament and knowledge. She felt, sometimes, that she was making her way in a thick forest where every tree was distinctive. Except that trees are almost never threatening, as some people are. One feeling that she learned to recognize in her body was *fear*. At first, the intensity of it almost immobilized her. But eventually she learned how it worked; her body told her to *flee!*, but when she thought a bit she recognized that she had other options. Her body could do things that it didn't seem to know it could do.

Sexual desire was another. She figured out that it was a primitive impulse, probably to ensure the continuation of the species. Yet in the culture in which she found herself, the feeling had been engulfed in taboos. She was intrigued by the different attitudes and behaviors exhibited within the drive to procreate. When conditions were right, sex was delightful. The feelings engulfed her, like the effects of alcohol, but without the wearisome aftereffects that drinking produced.

With Tim that night, she enjoyed watching and feeling him as he fell into the instinct-driven behavior, inexperienced as he was. If she could just persuade him to talk about it afterward!

By the next spring, she and Tim had become friends, sharing meals and walks in the snow when the wind wasn't too bad.

He was amused at her seeming naivety. "How was it right after your accident? Did you remember anything? Like who you were?"

She told him that it was months later before she could venture outside the hospital, simply because she did not recognize anything or anyone. The world was a great, buzzing confusion. Gradually, she learned to identify people with whom she had daily contact, and she learned how to converse with them.

But some things from her past had remained; she understood language, although many words were merely sounds for a long time. She felt things that she could not identify or respond to.

Gradually, the world around her began to make sense, to be somewhat predictable. And the world inside her brain also began to be recognizable.

Tim was fascinated by all this. To him, she was a foreigner, struck by all the little aspects of living in a secluded town huddled against the snow and cold. He enjoyed teaching her.

And he enjoyed being taught by her. Sex was a frequent pastime for them, and Daniele knew a good deal about it. Patient with his fumbling urgency, she persuaded him to pay attention to her as well as to his own impulses. Over time, she learned more about her own physical responses and how to experience the intensity that he seemed to enjoy so effortlessly.

When he was away visiting his family, she strolled the streets and the waterfront on the bay, watching people, exchanging greetings with the occasional locals whom she got to know.

Two

The warmth of the open fire made Daniele drowsy. She'd had two glasses of wine, sitting and watching the other patrons. She felt like smiling. She smiled at everyone who looked at her.

"Would you like some company?"

She hadn't noticed the man come into the room until he put a hand on the other chair next to her table. She lifted her glass and smiled.

"I'm Andrew," he said, sitting in the chair and signaling to the waitperson. "Are you waiting for someone?"

"For you," she said. It pleased her that she was learning the language of flirting.

Gray at the temples, no sign of baldness, clean shaven. He wore a business suit, but his shirt was open at the neck, without a tie. "Are you here for dinner, or do you just like a warm fire in this cold town?"

"It is pleasant," she said. "No, I've eaten already. I come here often in the evening." She smiled at him.

He ordered a gimlet—"Double," he told the waitperson.

Her pen poised: "Gin or vodka?"

"Vodka, of course. Up." He smiled at the waitperson and then at Daniele. "Never could understand why people put sweet lime juice into gin."

"Why?" asked Daniele.

"Gin is already sweet. It needs vermouth, or tonic water." He thought for a second. "Maybe fresh lime juice would work, but I was never tempted."

"You seem to have strong preferences." She studied him as one would study a specimen. *He's used to taking charge,* she thought. *It probably helps him persuade people to do what he wants.*

He didn't notice, but pulled a credit card from his pocket and laid it on the table.

"Passing through?" she asked.

"Sales rep," he said. "A sales rep is always just passing through."

"That must be a lonely life."

He looked carefully at her for the first time. She was dressed modestly but tastefully. *Not a hooker,* he decided.

"Sometimes," he replied.

He looked up when the waitperson returned with his drink. "Gracias," he said to her.

"What do you sell?" Daniele asked.

"Craft beers." He sipped from the glass and, satisfied, sipped again. "Not bad," he announced.

Leaning back in his chair, he asked, "What's a doll like you doing sitting by the fire alone?"

"Doll?" Her expression was bland.

He laughed. "Oh, I'm sorry, ma'am. No offence."

"Isn't a doll a kind of children's toy?" Daniele tried to process this new expression.

His face reddened. "Of course," he said. "It's just a term of endearment, like 'Honey'."

Her face still expressionless, she said, "Okay. I understand. I've just never been called a doll before."

He looked at her, trying to see if she were stringing him along. Then he grinned. "Okay," he said, "I get it. I apologize, Ms., uh—what do you call yourself?"

"Daniele," she answered, "but you had no way to know that, did you?"

"All right, *Daniele*," emphasizing the word, "can we start over? I didn't mean to offend you."

"I wasn't offended," she said.

His brow wrinkled. "You are—I hope you won't take this wrong—you are a very strange woman."

She smiled at him for the second time. "Perhaps. I'm here to observe."

He laughed, finished his gimlet, and put out his hand. "Daniele, I'm Andrew," he said. "What are you observing?"

She took his hand briefly. "People."

He caught the eye of the bartender and lifted his glass. To Daniele, he said, "I observe people, too. It's part of my job. I could have a master's in psychology, as much as I have learned about people."

"That's very interesting," she replied.

"You wouldn't believe some of the people I've worked with. Some of them—" he sniggered—"are real weirdos."

"What is that—'weirdos'?"

He frowned.

Just then the waitperson brought his drink. "You want another Pinot Grigio, Ms.?"

Daniele smiled at her. "I'm going to try one of Andrew's gimlets," she said.

"Hey," he said, pushing his glass toward her, "you can have a sip of mine. You know, just to see if you like it."

"I'm sure I will."

The woman gave Daniele a knowing look and left the table.

When her gimlet arrived, his was half gone. He lifted his glass. "To trying new things!"

Sweet-sour. Bite of vodka—a cheap vodka, she decided, *but okay.* She was feeling mellow, and made a mental note to herself: *Alcohol smooths out every experience. There will be a price to pay, I know, but right now I have a human in my sights. (Is that the right term?)*

"I guess," she said, just a bit slowly, "that your job presents many new things—right?"

"Right," he replied, "every contact means a new thing I have to deal with. Disgruntled employees, resistant bosses, confused bookkeepers."

"It must be very frustrating," she said.

He sighed deeply. "You know it."

"What do you do to relieve the frustration?" she asked, expressionless.

He looked down, smiling to himself. Then he looked up at her without speaking. *Hooker,* he thought. *She's a hooker, after all.*

"Do you have a family, Andrew?" she asked.

What kind of question is that? he asked himself. "Yes," he said, "wife and two kids. Who doesn't?"

"You don't get to see them very much." It was a statement.

He looked at her for a long time. Then he said, "Life on the road isn't easy."

"Do you miss them?"

His forehead squinched up into a frown. He didn't say anything. *Fucking bitch. I don't need this.*

"I'm sorry," she said softly. "That was imposing."

His expression softened, and he sighed deeply. "Y'know? This job is a bitch. I'm away from home three weeks out of every month. My wife is talking about a divorce. My kids don't know me."

The alcohol has gotten to him, too, she thought. "I'm sorry," she said softly.

He sipped his drink, then pointed to her glass. "What d'you think?"

"I like it," she said. "The vodka is a little bland for my taste, but I like the sweet-sour taste."

"The secret is in the Rose's Lime Juice. They've been making it the same way for years. Just the right amount of sweetness for a gimlet. No need for simple syrup, like they do with straight lime juice."

"Someone like you, you call on bars all the time, I suppose you get to know a lot about drinks." She began to feel sleepy from the alcohol.

Andrew chuckled. "You've had a snootful, haven't you?"

"Snootful?" Her brow wrinkled.

He laughed out loud. "You're somethin' else!"

"You mean I'm not what you expected. But what is 'snootful'?"

He put his hand on hers. "That just means that you've had a lot to drink, Honey."

"Daniele."

"Scuse me. Daniele."

"Yes, I have had a lot to drink," she said, her words carefully enunciated.

"You look tired. Why don't you let me take you someplace where you can rest a little." He stood up. "I've got a room right across the street. You can stretch out there for a few minutes." He extended his hand toward her.

Daniele looked up at him. "I don't want sex," she said.

Andrew appeared surprised at her bluntness, but grinned and passed it off. "Of course, Honey. You just need some rest."

She took his hand and stood up unsteadily. "I think I'm drunk." She giggled.

"You just need to rest for a few minutes."

This is not good, she thought. *He's expecting sex.* She said, "I uh, *je vais aux toilettes".*

For a moment he frowned, trying to interpret her French, but then he grinned. "Sure, Babe. Can you make it alone?"

Without responding to him, she made it toward the back of the restaurant where she knew the restrooms were. *I don't want to get hurt,* she thought as she walked, *and I don't want to hurt him, either. Better to leave.*

The exit was easy to find. Once outside, her head cleared a little, and she found her way to a back street, and eventually to home.

In the restaurant, Andrew waited a few minutes then paid the bill and left. It wasn't the first time he'd been stood up.

Walking home, Daniele's mind cleared, even though she still felt the effects of the alcohol. *This body of mine tends to want that feeling, the warmth—cozy, that's the feeling—even when it knows the probable result, which isn't in its best interest.*

"I'm here to observe" had been her mantra ever since *the fall,* and likely long before that. It's hard to remember—*is that a term for us?*—when I was not she. *Am I becoming human?*

That night in her bed alone, she thought of Tim with a new kind of feeling. She missed him. She felt somehow protective of him. She wanted to do something for him. *But he needs to learn more about living,* she thought. *He needs to be with other people.*

Three

D aniele had known physical pain only once before, when Mack, the man who had abandoned her in this little town, beat her when he found out about her real identity.

They had been on a late-fall vacation, driving up from Detroit where they had met only weeks before. Mack was outgoing and seemingly tolerant of her peculiarities, so she had told him in a roundabout way how she had occupied this body of a woman who had just died from a fall down some stairs in Dallas. "I am," she had said, "the same person, but only with some memory lapses. I've lost her connections to others, so it's as though I've begun with a *blank slate,* as you call it."

At first he had laughed at her. "I always thought you were from another world," he said. You're like no other woman I've known."

But she sensed that he didn't really believe her, that she was kidding him. That troubled her; it was not in her nature—her real nature or her nature as Daniele, the woman—to lie to anyone. She had recognized that humans often lied, but it didn't make sense to contaminate communication, which was often difficult as it was.

"I've tried to be true to her," she had said to him, "true to who she was, even though there are large gaps in her memory. As I've told you many times, I'm here to observe."

The reality of what she was saying slowly sank in. His response then was sudden and violent. "But then you're not even human!" he shouted. "You're like a robot! I've been fucking a fucking robot!"

Stunned by his vehemence, she tried to mollify the situation. She smiled, and she talked about other things, and after a time his expression softened. But it changed the relationship.

Daniele spent many hours trying to process what had happened. She knew, from very deep inside—deeper than her human mind—that such situations were not rare among humans. As an individual, she worked hard at the task.

Mack had been an energetic lover, enticing her to please him in different ways. He had never asked what he could do to please her. That wasn't unusual in her experience with men. Courting her with attention and flattery, they made her feel valued, even precious. It seemed to her that many men, so differently from their behavior when trying to coax her into bed, once sex had begun focused only on their own sensations.

Following her revelation to him, Mack lost the gentleness he had previously used to initiate sexual intimacy. His cursory, even rough, foreplay became automatic, as though he was, indeed, "having sex with a robot." He became robot-like.

Daniele took it in along with all the other information she absorbed about human beings. The human in her as Daniele was disappointed; that feeling, too, was filed away.

She was here to observe.

Mack finally blew up in anger over some misunderstanding, striking her in the face and arms as she tried to fend off his blows. "I've had it with you—whatever you are!" he roared, and packed his clothing, got into his car and left.

Daniele moved into another, smaller apartment. She had no money problems; there was always a bank account arranged in her name wherever she went.

Where she lived at any time wasn't very important, as long as people were nearby. Her larger purpose never changed. She was learning what being human meant. And she was learning what a woman thinks and feels.

Four

Lying awake and alone in her bed was Daniele's time to piece together what was a growing understanding of being human. She knew, of course, that this situation was taking place all over the earth. Other parts of her reality were dealing with other human interactions. She didn't know how long—in human terms—she would be occupying Daniele's body.

She knew that humans have limited life-spans, and accidents and diseases often shorten even those. Daniele had been a young woman when she suffered the accident, and since then she had lived about a dozen years. When her body finally succumbed to some life-taking event, there would be another vehicle suitable for study.

She thought that she could learn a lot more from Tim. He was young and open to her—as Daniele. She felt his enthusiasm, and somehow it pleased her. She wondered how she might guide his growth.

Was there an ideal human? What was the potential within him that needed only encouragement to blossom into maturity? As Daniele, she felt a kind of life-flow toward a more effective, productive humanity. It seemed that Tim had more of that potential than Daniele had. Why was that? If she were here only to observe, why did she feel that life-flow, that river of humanness as something to be nurtured?

Why did it trouble Daniele sometimes *to feel*? The True Nature within her mind had no sense of right and wrong, no yearning except to learn. How would being Daniele change that?

In these reveries, watching the patterns of light changing on the ceiling of her room, she sometimes remembered vaguely other people she had encountered since becoming Daniele (was she really Daniele?).

Walter—a man whom she had searched for and finally found, for what purpose she never discovered, except that he knew something about the woman Daniele, felt something that for some reason appealed to the being that lived in her body.

He had known about us, had met several people in whom we resided for a time. Only when he had to deal personally with them did he withdraw. He seemed not able to integrate his feelings about the original Daniele with the present Daniele. He was not violent, like Mack, but he was unable to process the difference emotionally.

Something inside Daniele still felt drawn to Walter. The other Daniele must have felt strongly about him before. Was that *love?*

Had she come to love Tim? How did he feel about her?

Five

"I missed you!" Tim said, with that cute grin of his. *'Cute?'* she thought. *Where did I learn that word?*

"I hope your visit with your parents went well," she responded.

"Yes," he said, "I get along with them better than I did when I lived with them. My dad even talked about my getting back into NMU."

"That would be wonderful. You have a lot of potential, and you won't make it real by bagging groceries for middle-aged women."

They both laughed.

"What is 'making it real?' he asked. "You sound like a philosopher," *Cute grin.*

"Everyone has some kind of potential—like a plant has the potential to become a flower."

"Wow," he said. "You really are a philosopher."

She smiled at him. "Remember? I'm here to observe—and to learn."

Tim chuckled. "So your potential is to become a human?"

Daniele was dumbfounded. "What do you mean?" *What does he know about me?*

Flustered, he tried to find words. "I—I don't know. You just seem to be more *regular* than you were when I met you." He laughed nervously. "Like you were just born ten years ago, and you're becoming—I don't know!"

She was silent for a long time.

"I'm sorry," he said, putting a hand on her arm, "I didn't mean that."

"Yes, you did," she said, covering his hand with her own, "and it's true."

They were seated on her little sofa, and she turned her body to better face him. "Tim," she said, "you need to know something about me."

"I know I love you," he said, his voice strained.

She kissed him, a gentle, lingering kiss.

"Daniele," she said, "was a woman who died suddenly in a fall down some stairs ten years ago."

His eyes, at first uncomprehending, widened. "What do you mean?" he asked.

"I—I have lived in Daniele's body since just after she died. I have been *becoming* Daniele ever since."

He shook his head and looked across the room.

"Tim, I know this is hard to understand. I'm not sure I understand it either."

"Then who are you?" He studied her face, as though seeing her for the first time. "I don't get it."

"I know," she said. "I—we—are here to observe, as I've said to you many times. We're here to learn what it is to be human. You see, we are not human, not like you."

"Where do you come from?" His face looked as though he were about to cry.

"I can't answer that in a way that would make sense to you," she said, holding his hand tightly. "We don't even have a *presence* that you could see or hear. It's only by living inside a human body that we can communicate with humans, and that's how we study what 'being human' means."

Tim seemed out of breath. He looked down at her hand on his, and she relaxed her grip. He didn't withdraw it, but looked instead at her face. Tears welled up in his eyes.

"I love you, too, Tim," she said softly. "I'm not sure what that means, but that's how I feel. Maybe that's what love is—*feeling*. Outside of this body, I don't think I have ever experienced it."

"But," he said hoarsely, "a minute ago I said I love you. Now I don't know what that means. Who do I love? If you're not Daniele, then *who do I love?* I thought I loved a woman named Daniele, but I know now that she's dead. Who are you?"

She embraced him as hard as she could. At first, he was tense but not resisting her, and then gradually his body relaxed into her embrace. He put his arms around her and began to sob.

After a long time, he fished in his pocket and drew out a handkerchief. Without removing his head from her shoulder, he blew his nose.

Then he laughed. "Sorry," he said.

They parted. Daniele felt tears run down her own cheeks. She took his handkerchief from him and wiped her eyes.

"Love," she said, "is just as big a mystery to me as it is to you. I don't even know who I am, except that I feel like I'm Daniele."

She drew back a little to see his face. "When you say you're Tim, who are you, really? We aren't the same, you and I, but are we really different?" She laughed softly, "Am I human—yet?"

He grinned. "You sure feel like a human to me."

"This is a lot for you to take in," she said. "It's a lot for me to take in."

They sat for a long time, feeling their individual feelings.

Then she said, "Tim, I've been thinking for a while now, that I may not be in Daniele's body forever, or even for however long she lives. I know that someday I'll not be here like this."

She sighed. "That's hard to think about. But isn't it hard to think about death anyway? How do you think about your own death? When you won't any longer be Tim?"

He shrugged. "I guess it's the same thing, isn't it?"

"I don't know."

"Tim," she said after a long time, "would you promise me something? I know that neither of us can promise we'll always be here, or that we'll always love each other."

He frowned, and began to say something. She put her hand on his arm again. "Tim, please promise me that, no matter what happens between us, you'll go back to college. I don't care what you study, just become your potential! Does that make sense?"

He nodded. "Will you come with me?"

She thought for a while. "No," she said softly. "You need to do it for yourself."

He shook his head.

"Do it because I love you. Does that help?"

After a while, he nodded his head.

They had a week together, pretending that it would be forever. Then he gave notice to his boss at the grocery store, packed up his clothing, and left Charlevoix.

Daniele strolled along the waterfront by the bay, and sat beside the fireplace in the dark restaurant by the drawbridge, and thought about being human.

The End

Harmony

"It's harmony," the guy said. "I believe that the secret to all good relationships is harmony." He grinned at Katherine. "Simple as that."

"But that's *too* simple," she protested. "A man could be stringing me along, and saying all the right words, and I could be taken in by that, when really all he's trying to do is further his own agenda. The harmony I might think is between us has nothing to do with how different we really are."

I guess I was grinning too, because when she glanced at me for support, she frowned. "Tim, say something!"

I leaned past her to look over at the guy. "Depends on what you call harmony, doesn't it? People can be polite to each other, trying to smooth out the edges of what they really feel, trying to get along." I wasn't sure just what he was getting at, but I suspected that he had something more specific in mind.

"I'm sorry," he said, laughing. "I guess I think about this so much I forget that other people haven't been inside my head just before I speak." He stuck out his hand. "I'm Harry."

Katherine and I introduced ourselves—first names only (who knows who this guy really is or what he's up to?)—and shook hands with him. I noticed that his hand was cold, but the gesture seemed hearty.

We were sitting on a park bench looking out over the Grand Canyon, when Harry had sat down after giving us a polite questioning look, as if to say, "Okay if

I join you?" and we had both nodded. He gazed out at the spectacle and sighed deeply. "Just looking at this, it resonates with you, doesn't it?" he had said. "Brings people together."

"Mmm," said Katherine, smiling quickly at him and then looking back out into space.

"I feel that," I said. "My wife and I can see the same thing and we know we're having the same feelings."

I was sending him a message without really thinking about it, letting him know that she belonged to me, sort of.

He got it, and caught my eye for just that instant, letting *me* know he heard me. "You're in harmony," he said. He repeated the remark, "The secret to all good relationships is harmony."

Katherine had reacted to him somehow. She didn't trust him. There was an edge to her voice. "I'd say the word is 'trust'."

Katherine's a writer, and she values precise meanings to words. We have frequent discussions about the meanings of words we use with each other. I tend to be a little sloppy sometimes, using a word that seems close enough to what I mean, if I think she'll understand me. When she said "trust," I knew she meant that we trust each other to clarify when we need to. That's the give and take of a good relationship.

"Yes," he said. "I see that. Trust is the background. You have to have that. But what I'm referring to is something deeper. You can't manufacture harmony. You can create trust, just by keeping your word and talking about your differences. But *harmony* is what brought you together in the first place."

She looked down at her hands. "You may be right." It was a dismissal. She didn't think he knew what he was talking about.

The guy intrigued me. There was something different about him. I had the feeling he was playing with ideas, trying to understand something that I've wondered about myself sometimes. But he reminded me of *Good Will Hunting,* that old movie about a mathematical genius who had difficulty understanding about relationships.

I had read some of the books by neuroscientists on the subject of mirror neurons, which are supposed to behave the same way whether one is eating a cookie or only watching someone else eat a cookie. According to some researchers, the effect demonstrates how people experience empathy.

"Tell me," I said to him, "what this 'harmony' is. What do you mean by 'harmony'?

He stood up and came around to my end of the bench. I moved over to let him sit down.

"You know what harmony is in music," he said.

It surprised me. How could he know what I know about music? "Okay," I said, waiting for him to continue.

"Notes that seem to fit with others just naturally, that we sense even if we've not had any training in music theory." He had a slight smile on his face. "I think you've had that experience."

I nodded. "Perfect fourth, perfect fifth, octave, triads." I thought of the song "Hallelujah" by Leonard Cohen, *"...it goes like this, the fourth, the fifth, the minor fall, and the major lift ..."*

"Yes. The interval of a fifth puts one note in relationship to another as three is to two. That's harmony."

Katherine sighed. I put my hand on her knee to acknowledge her impatience.

I said, "You're saying that the mathematical basis of Western music can be applied to personal relationships?"

"Makes sense, doesn't it? I mean, humans are seekers of patterns, even when we're not conscious of it. Similar patterns are active in our brains."

When I glanced at his eyes, I felt something strange. You know how people often looked in those old photographs from the nineteenth century, where their eyes had this weird, blank look? That came from them moving their eyes during the long exposures that were needed for photographs then. Not that this guy's eyes were just white—his pupils were pretty wide, actually, the irises an ordinary bronze color. But he had a kind of faraway look in his eyes.

Katherine stood up. "I'm going back to our room," she said.

"I'll be right there," I said to her, and turned to the guy. "Interesting idea."

We nodded to each other, and I followed Katherine.

Later in our room, she said, "That guy gave me the creeps."

I laughed. "Yeah. He was kinda strange."

Our dinner reservation was in an hour, so we stretched out on the bed and read for a while. The strange man was forgotten.

The next morning, however, we were in the café eating breakfast when he approached us again. "Morning, Tim, Katherine," he said as though he had known us for years. "May I join you?"

Katherine looked away, but I answered, "Sure," and gestured toward an empty chair at our table.

Just as he sat down, the waitperson appeared, and he ordered coffee and a scone.

After she left, he said, "I had a feeling that you were uncomfortable yesterday." He was looking directly at Katherine, who turned back and even smiled quickly.

"Technical talk doesn't interest me much," she said.

"I apologize," he replied. "I know I get carried away sometimes when I think I'm on the trail of a new idea."

"Are you a scientist?" I asked.

"Not exactly," he said.

"You sounded like a music professor or something."

"I observe," he said simply.

"I'm curious," I said. "May I be frank?"

He nodded. "Of course."

"Why did you pick us to connect with yesterday? You're obviously not a typical con man, trying to get a buck off some tourists."

"And I didn't convince you that I was just a fellow tourist, trying to be friendly."

"Your observation about harmony. That wasn't just an idle conversation starter. You had a purpose."

He grinned. "You're very observant." Taking a deep breath and letting it out slowly, he said, "You said you're curious. I'm also very curious about people. I caught something from you yesterday—when you came out of the curio shop—you were talking to your wife about Michael Polanyi. I felt a connection."

It caught me in my midsection. I suddenly felt as though my brain were being dissected. "You know Michael Polanyi?"

"Tacit knowledge." His grin seemed pasted on.

" 'We can know more than we can tell.' Yes." I looked at him closely. "What's that got to do with harmony?"

He smiled. "That's what I felt—harmony—between us." He made a little gesture toward Katherine. "Katherine said the secret of a close relationship is more like trust."

I saw out of the corner of my eye that she was now paying attention.

"Isn't trust more *explicit* knowledge?" He had this funny little smile on his lips.

"And you're saying that harmony is more like tacit knowledge."

Harry laughed. "I don't know. I'm trying out ideas."

Katherine made a little gesture of impatience. "What's this about tacit and explicit knowledge? I'm not following you at all."

I put my hand on hers. "Michael Polanyi proposed that we have some kinds of knowledge that we cannot tell someone else in words."

Harry opened his hands on the table. "Tacit knowledge is that which we know that we cannot tell. Think about riding a bicycle. You know that you can do it. Could you tell someone how to do it?"

"I'd have to show them," she said. "It's about balance and feeling what the bicycle is doing."

"They could watch you do it," he said, "but to *know how*, *themselves*, they'd have to do it, and learn the physical sensations in their body. Could you describe that?"

She frowned and looked at me.

"But isn't *trust* also tacit knowledge?" I was thinking that we were getting away from what he really wanted to talk about. "I have a feeling that I'm trusting you but that Katherine isn't. I don't know how to describe it, exactly, but we all know the word. What's trust *really mean?*"

Katherine frowned again. She wasn't comfortable revealing her private feelings to this man, especially since she didn't trust him.

I touched her hand again. "Sorry, I shouldn't speak for you, should I?"

Harry just watched us, looking from one to the other.

Her eyes were alert. She was rising to the challenge. "I hear," she said to him, "the idea that *harmony* is a tacit thing. We listen to music and we don't hear the patterns, we hear the music. Under our conscious sensations the patterns of harmony affect us, even if we can't put that effect into words. I might respond, 'It sounds wonderful,' and that may be as close as I can get to describing it. Right?"

"Exactly!" he said. "You've got it. But the harmony I'm talking about is about relationships. I *think*," and he made little quotation marks in the air, "that we *vibrate* in harmony with some people and not with others. When you said you don't trust me—"

She broke in, "I didn't tell you—"

"No," he said, smiling, "Tim here told me that, and he apologized for revealing it. But I sensed it, just as he did, before we got into it. Actually," and his smile turned into a grin, "when you first used the word yesterday I knew you didn't trust me. Our vibrations did not harmonize."

We all laughed, but that odd feeling from yesterday stirred inside me. I wondered if it was some kind of tacit knowledge about this man, something different from harmony. His eyes seemed more normal this morning, but that feeling I had ...

He sat back in his chair and sipped his coffee. "I once heard someone say that 'it's all vibrations.' We see, we hear, we touch, and everything is vibrational. Maybe life is nothing but vibrations."

Katherine got this little smile in the corner of her mouth. "I've heard that, too," she said. "I was in a community once, a spiritual community, that talked about that and used that word. It explained a lot to me at the time, even though I didn't really understand it."

"Interesting," he said. "Maybe my idea isn't so new, after all."

"Hmm." I said. "Would you tell us something about yourself? You've got me curious."

Harry laughed. "There isn't much I can tell you. I have a memory problem, you see."

"You sure don't seem to have a memory problem."

"It's just that I can't remember much beyond the past couple of years." He ran his fingers through his hair. "They tell me I had an accident."

That odd feeling hit me in my gut. I was suddenly nervous. "I'm sorry," I said, "but I'm not feeling well. I hope you'll excuse me." I stood up. "Katherine, stay if you like. I just want to lie down for a while."

"No," she said, standing. "I'm going with you."

Harry stood also. "I'm sorry. I hope I haven't said anything to upset you."

"No, no," I said. "I'm just a little dizzy. Maybe it's the altitude."

We left him standing at the table, looking troubled. Katherine took my arm as we left the restaurant and walked back to our room. She kept looking at me but said nothing.

In the room, I lay down on the bed, and she stood over me. "What's going on, Tim?" she asked.

"You know, I'm not sure, but that guy is not like us."

She frowned. "Well, yes, I felt that, too. But what do you mean?"

I breathed deeply for a moment. "I've read about people who are *inhabited*, I think is the word, by something."

She laughed. "Sweetie, you're delirious. Maybe it is the altitude that's got you."

I stared at the ceiling.

I could see in the corner of my eye that her expression changed. "Tim, does he remind you of someone in your past?"

Looking at her, I said, "Well, as a matter of fact, before you and I met, I was on a cruise ship—"

"With some other woman." Her eyes laughed.

"Well, yes. Before you. I was sitting in a little lounge, listening to a woman playing the piano, something by Clara Schumann. Afterward, I struck up a conversation with her, and she affected me the same way Harry did."

A smile played around her lips. "You *vibrated together?—in harmony?*"

"No, it wasn't like that," I said, chuckling. "It was as though—well, she said she had a memory problem, too. Maybe that's it. She couldn't remember her earlier life."

"And you think she and Harry are—how did you put it?—*inhabited?*"

I managed a smile. "At the time I felt like she was, like, *lurking* in her body. She could play classical music really well, although she said she only plays one or two composers. Didn't make sense to me. A musician as good as she was must have had years of training and practice. But the way she talked, she had started playing only a few years before. There was this—this *hollow* feeling about her. After we talked, I didn't go back to the lounge. It was weird."

Katherine sat beside me on the bed. Stroking my forehead, she said, "Well, we are checking out of this hotel in a couple of hours. We can avoid that guy before we leave. I'm ready to head home anyway."

She was quiet while we gathered our things and packed up to leave. I had opened the door to our room when she put a hand on my arm and closed the door again. "Tim," she said, putting her arms around me, "I need you to know that this is really me. I'm Katherine, your wife, and I can remember my childhood. I was only part of a person until I met you, but I was real. And I'm real now, inside and out. You and I do harmonize together."

She kissed me passionately, and we went through the door with all our baggage.

The End

Songs

Jane smiled as she pushed through the door to the *Easy Goin'* and heard the old Nancy Sinatra recording of "These Boots are Made for Walkin'" rising barely over the noise of the bar. She had a date with Donna, her friend from work, to talk about men.

Donna, her back to the door, was talking and laughing with a guy sitting next to her at the bar. Disappointment nudged at Jane's midsection. She sighed but went on, taking the seat on the other side of Donna. "Hey," she said.

Donna turned and grinned at her. "Hey."

The guy leaned forward to see Jane. Smiling, he said, "I'm Jackson."

Jackson was younger than the two women. His face carried that week's growth of dark beard that seemed to be the standard look on men these days. Jane wasn't fond of the look; it reminded her of someone who had just returned from a fishing trip in Canada. She had convinced her ex, Jeff, to keep his face cleanly shaved, at least until their relationship began showing signs of weakness. She hadn't seen him in several weeks, and imagined that he was reverting to type. Managing a smile for Jackson, she ordered a cosmo from the woman behind the bar.

"Donna told me that you two needed to talk about things," Jackson said, still leaning forward to see Jane's face. "Don't mind me. I just like to talk. I can move away, give you some privacy."

Donna touched her friend's hand. "You want to go back to a booth?"

"Yeah," said Jane softly, swiveling on the barstool.

"Thank you," Donna said to Jackson, and the two women made their way through the crowd to a booth.

Jackson watched them go, then ordered another drink.

"Okay, Love," said Donna. "what's going on?"

With a weak grin, Jane said, "You know." She sighed. "I miss 'im."

"You deserve more than Jeff, Love."

"But I used to feel he was something special. He treated me like *I* was special. For a while I thought *'This could be The One'*."

"You need someone like—" Donna nodded her head toward Jackson, "like *him,* to take your mind off Jeff."

"You think he's different?"

Donna grinned. "I do. In more ways than one."

They both looked toward the bar. Jackson had turned around on the stool and was facing them. He saluted with his glass.

"You meet him just now?" asked Jane.

Donna nodded. "As soon as I sat down, he appeared on the stool next to me."

"He's cute."

"Actually," said Donna, "he's pretty smart, too. Started talking about emotions and the amygdala."

"What, is he some kind of scientist?"

"I don't think so. He was a little vague when I asked him the same thing. He said he is 'here to observe'."

Jane smiled. "You want to go back over there before he gets away?"

Donna shook her head. "I'm here for you today. Men are a dime a dozen in this place."

Donna played the field. For her, men were recreational playmates. She had told Jane that she'd never fall in love. "Love is painful."

Jane finished her drink. "If he knows about the amygdala, maybe he can tell me why I can't let go of Jeff."

"You think it's just hormonal?" Donna grinned and then turned to glance toward the bar.

"I don't know. Jeff's a nice enough guy. He just can't keep his dick in his pants. I can't handle that. I need somebody I can count on, someone who considers me first."

In a few moments they were interrupted by Jackson, who appeared beside them carrying a tray of three drinks. "Noticed you were out," he said, and waited for a response.

Donna moved over to let him sit next to her. "You're very gallant," she said.

Jackson placed the drinks on the table and sat down. "I don't want to be pushy," he said, propping the tray against the side of the booth.

"Of course you don't," said Donna, smiling. She looked over at Jane and raised her eyebrows.

Jane shrugged.

Jackson picked up his drink. "As a man," he said with a little grin, "I'm confused. What is it about sex that gets in the way—sometimes—of love?"

Jane and Donna exchanged a glance that made use of eyebrows, as though to ask, "Is he for real?"

"Are you serious?" asked Donna.

"They are two different things," said Jane. "Love is more important."

"But both of them involve a lot of the same hormonal responses." Jackson suddenly seemed younger. "Lust and affection—both release dopamine and serotonin."

"Is that true?" asked Jane.

Jackson shrugged. "What I read."

Donna picked up her phone and began touching the display. After a moment, reading from the phone, she said, "Oxytocin is known as the cuddle hormone." She paused. "The heart has receptors for oxytocin and it helps heart cells regenerate and heal from any stress-induced damage."

Jane smiled at Donna. "You think?" she asked softly.

Jackson looked from one to the other. "Another hormone."

Jane's face became serious. "Chemistry can't explain all of human relationships."

"Go ahead," said Donna, "tell him what your question is."

Jane looked down at her drink. "Hypothetically," she said, "just suppose someone used to be in love with somebody, but isn't any more, but she—or he—can't seem to forget that somebody."

Jackson looked at the ceiling and stroked his chin whiskers. "Well, hypothetically—what is he or she trying to forget? The sex or the love?"

Jane blushed.

"I mean," he said, "this person is no longer in love, but maybe he or she just wants something she lost, but not the object of her affection, as the song used to go."

"His or hers," corrected Donna.

"His or hers." Jackson turned and signaled the bartender.

"Are we different? Donna asked. "Men and women?"

Jackson grinned. "Don't ask me!"

"Why? Aren't you a man?" asked Jane.

"Are you gay?" asked Donna.

Jackson's grin stayed on his face. "I'm not sure how to answer that." He looked down at his shirt. "By all appearances..."

"That doesn't answer the question," said Donna.

Jane frowned. "But that just complicates it more. This *person* isn't gay."

"Sorry," said Donna. "I shouldn't have brought that into the conversation. I'm just curious."

"Let's just say, I find you two ladies very attractive." He turned as the waiter approached, and held up three fingers. Then he turned back. "From what I've read, we all have the same hormones in us—testosterone, estrogen, ...

"In varying extents," said Jane.

Donna sipped from her drink. "But love requires something more than lust. Lust is 'gimme, gimme, gimme. Love is wanting to give." She looked up. "Isn't it?"

Jane laughed. "On the nailhead."

"Simple as that?" asked Jackson. "A while ago I saw an old man sitting up against the building with his shopping cart beside him. This woman dropped something in his paper cup and just walked on. Was that love?"

Jane nodded. "Yeah, a kind of love."

"Well, how does that resemble the kind of love you used to feel about—what's his name?"

"I was speaking hypothetically."

"Okay," Jackson admitted. "This *person* used to feel."

"Involves intimacy." Jane was feeling the alcohol. She remembered Jeff, back in their early days, hovering over her, sensitive to her moods, touching her gently on the cheek.

"Intimacy." Jackson paused, as though in thought. "Is that some of that 'gimme, gimme, gimme'?"

Donna laughed, but Jane's brow furrowed. "I don't—" she began.

Donna interrupted her. "The woman who put something in the old man's cup didn't feel intimacy with him—probably didn't know him at all, just felt like he was someone in need."

"Didn't know him at all?" Jackson grinned. "Do you know that for a fact?"

Donna blushed. "Well, I assume she didn't. She might not have, and still wanted to give him something."

"Intimacy," said Jackson. "You think she didn't know him, so she didn't feel intimacy. Then what's intimacy?"

"Physical intimacy," said Jane. "Being physically close, touching somebody."

"She didn't want to touch him," said Jackson.

"No."

"Let's be hypothetical. Let's say he was her father. Would she have wanted intimacy with him then?"

Both women were silent. Jane looked at her hands.

After a moment, Donna said, "This is getting way off the subject."

"I'm sorry," said Jackson. "I'm just trying to understand."

Jane's face was a mask.

"Okay," said Donna, "forget about the old man on the sidewalk. For me, physical intimacy usually—not always, but usually—includes at least a bit of lust. But intimacy is not always physical. Jane and I—" she gestured toward her friend, "are pretty intimate, but it isn't physical."

The three of them laughed.

"Other than frequent hugs," Jane added, and they laughed again.

"Oxytocin," said Jackson. "What you read just now."

The two women exchanged a glance. Then Donna said, "Let's get back to Jane's hypothetical question."

"I'm no expert," Jackson said, "but maybe this *person* is missing the intimacy with the guy she no longer is in love with."

"Maybe," admitted Jane.

Jackson looked at Donna. "What do you think?"

Donna shrugged. "Maybe." She looked toward Jane. "Jane's a softy."

Jackson leaned back in the booth. "But what do *I* know?" he asked.

"You seem to have a lot of answers for someone who, as you told me a while ago, you're 'just here to observe'." Donna finished her drink.

Jane, looking at Jackson, asked, "What do you think about the question?"

Jackson grinned. "I have very limited experience in these things."

"I bet," said Donna.

Jane leaned forward. "Do men want intimacy? Or just sex?"

Jackson's face became serious, and he paused before answering. "I don't know," he said. "I haven't talked with many men."

"*Observed* was the word you used." Donna held his gaze.

The three of them were silent for a time.

"Tell me something," Donna said. "Why did you bring up that business about the old man on the sidewalk?"

Jackson drained the remaining drops from his glass. "Just curious," he said quietly. "Why she just walked away from him."

"She didn't want to get involved," said Jane.

"With her own father?" Jackson frowned.

"What?" exclaimed Donna. "How do you know that?"

Jackson looked down, and then held up his glass to signal the waitperson.

"You said 'hypothetical'," said Jane. "You know those people?"

"Just guessed."

"No you didn't just guess." Donna pushed her glass out toward him. Her face challenged him.

"I'm not comfortable with this," Jane said, slouching back in the corner. She remembered her father calling her "Princess" and always treating her like one.

He glanced at Jane, then looked across the room toward the bar.

"You know those people?" asked Donna.

He nodded. "Just trying to understand."

"What are you trying to understand?" Donna asked.

"Love," he said simply.

"This is the weirdest conversation I've ever had in a bar," said Donna.

"With a stranger, at that," added Jane.

"I'm not sure any of us are sober enough for this," said Donna. "This isn't just bar talk."

He looked up at her. "What should it be, instead?"

"Flirting."

"What's flirting?"

Donna gave a little laugh. "It's a game," she said. "It's what people do in a bar. They spar with each other, try to keep the upper hand."

"What wins the game?"

"Sex, on your own terms."

He looked at Jane, who was still almost cowering in the corner. "Is that why you're uncomfortable?"

She looked at him without responding.

"I'm sorry," he said, "I thought we were talking about love."

The waiter brought their drinks.

"You're a very strange man," said Donna.

Jackson leaned closer and spoke softly. "Where I come from, sex doesn't exist—and your *love* is a mystery to me."

"You *are* gay," said Donna.

"No."

"Then I don't understand."

His shoulders sagged, and he smiled wryly. "We don't reproduce that way."

Both women frowned. Jane sat up. "Where do you come from?" she asked softly.

"I'm here to observe."

Donna said, "C'mon. What are you trying to say? You're from outer space?"

He smiled. "I don't know how to answer that so you could understand."

"You're from another planet, but you look just like us—like men on Earth."

He shook his head. "It's not that simple."

Jane leaned toward him. "So how do you reproduce?"

"Songs."

"Songs?" Donna's brow furrowed.

"It's the closest thing I can think of that you might understand."

Jane said, "I don't understand that at all."

"You don't have sex." said Donna.

He chuckled. "No." Then he took a breath. "Well, frankly, in *this* form" and gesturing toward himself, "I do—I *can*."

Donna laughed out loud. "That's—that's the most original line I have ever heard!"

He leaned closer, and both women echoed his action.

"I am *inhabiting* the body of a human who died."

Both women suddenly leaned away from him, shock showing on their faces.

"I'm sorry," he said, his voice still soft, "no human has been harmed. We take on this form just so we can observe."

None of them spoke for a long time. Then Jane asked gently, "How did he die—how did you die?"

"Brain aneurism."

A long pause.

Then Donna spoke, her voice shaking slightly. "So you're an alien being from outer space somewhere, occupying the body of some guy—"

"Who was he?" asked Jane.

"His name was Jackson. He died in the hospital. Nobody could locate his family."

Donna frowned. "Why are you here?"

Jackson shrugged. "We're not here to harm anybody. We just want to observe."

"How many of you are here?" asked Donna.

He shrugged again. "I don't know how to answer that."

About the old man and his daughter," she said. "You could tell just by watching?"

He nodded. "I could tell."

"You can read minds?"

"Not exactly."

"What are *songs?*" Jane looked concerned.

He smiled. "That's how we reproduce. It's the closest thing I can think of to describe it to you."

"Songs."

"Yes."

"*Intimate* songs?"

He smiled at her.

Donna leaned toward him. "Can you sing me a song?"

He shook his head, still smiling.

She leaned closer and whispered, "But you could have sex with me."

"Donna!" Jane exclaimed softly.

His expression didn't change.

Donna smiled. "A way for you to observe."

Jane leaned back. "I don't believe this."

"An experiment for both of us," Donna said, still looking at him.

"Donna," said Jane, "you can't be serious!"

Donna sat back and looked at her. "Maybe I could answer your question about love and sex." She looked back at Jackson. "You said you *could.*"

"Only sex," he said. "Not love."

She looked down at her hands. "Maybe love is overrated."

Jane looked at her sadly.

Donna glanced back at her quickly, then looked away. "I'm not sure what love is," she said to her hands. "And I can't have a *song* ..."

"Oh, Donna." Jane reached for her hand. She really wanted to hug her friend, reassure her that she deserved love.

Jackson looked from one to the other. Finally, he said, "I think I'm learning something."

Jane retreated to her corner again.

Donna finished her drink. "I'm sorry," she said, glancing at Jane. "My friend and I wanted to have a conversation, but I think we've spoiled it. Jackson, thank you for the drinks, but maybe later..."

Jackson looked from one to the other. "Of course," he said. "I'm intruding. Maybe later." He got out of the booth and picked up the tray he'd left on the floor. "I'll be around," he said to Donna, and walked away.

Donna looked at Jane. "You okay?"

"I'm sorry," Jane replied.

"Hey, don't apologize. I'm the one who invited him."

"It just felt like the same old game," Jane said. "Not what I was in the mood for."

"I think he's full of baloney anyway."

"You could have sex with him? All his talk about being something from—being an *alien?*"

"I don't know," Donna said. "For a minute there—" She laughed. "It could be a kick."

Jane smiled and shook her head.

"What he said, about maybe you are just missing the intimacy you had with Jeff. Does that sound true?"

"Maybe. Jeff could be really gentle."

Neither spoke for a few moments, then Donna asked, "You want another drink?"

"No. I can't think straight now as it is." She paused, and looked at her friend. "Donna, what he said about songs—"

"How they reproduce."

"Yeah. That sounds—"

"Wonder what it means."

"Doesn't it remind you, though, of what love feels like?"

"A song?"

"Yeah. You know, everybody used to sing love songs. There's that feeling you get about somebody."

Donna smiled. "You are so sentimental. I love that about you, though, you know it?"

"You're not sentimental." Jane returned her smile.

"He said he couldn't sing a song for me." She laughed. "It'd probably be in some alien language I couldn't understand anyway."

"Maybe it's like they don't even touch to reproduce."

Donna chuckled. "Now *that* doesn't sound like much fun."

"It was kinda sweet, though."

"I think he was handing us a line, actually," said Donna, wiping a wet spot from the table.

"You looked like you believed him."

Donna grinned at her. "Not really. He *was* almost charming."

"But you shut him down."

"I just remembered why we're here," Donna said. "He had us way off track."

"Thank you."

They sat and looked at each other for a while. Then Jane said, "He took my mind off of Jeff."

"Oh?"

"I keep thinking about *songs*."

"Okay, say more."

Jane toyed with her bar napkin, folding it and unfolding it. "Somehow that appealed to me."

Donna waited for her to continue.

Jane gave a little laugh. "Maybe I'm being silly," she said, "or maybe I just listened to too many love songs that my mother used to play all the time. Tony Bennett, Frank Sinatra ..."

"Boy, you do go back a long way."

Jane smiled. "I guess I'm just an old romantic."

"Maybe. Yes, you are."

"Long before I knew what sex was, I absorbed romance."

"So maybe it isn't intimacy you miss, it's romance?" Donna reached across the table to take her hand. "That's okay, Love."

Jane laughed quietly. "They aren't the same, are they?"

"Maybe they are—or maybe they go hand in hand."

"Wish I could have thought of that while Jackson was here."

"Why?"

"Maybe that would be closer to his *songs*."

"If he's real."

"I think he's real," Jane said.

Donna raised an eyebrow. "An *alien*."

"I don't know. But he touched me, somehow."

Donna smiled. "He said he's here to observe. Maybe you could teach him something."

The two women smiled at each other and began collecting their purses to leave.

The End

Stanley

One

He felt something in his chest, and rolled over on the old mattress. The smelly blanket had pulled away from him on one side, and he struggled to cover himself again. He couldn't open his eyes.

The whiff of stale wood smoke awakened him. The sky was beginning to lighten. His stomach complained. Sitting up, he looked around. His campfire gave no heat, only a wisp of cold smoke.

Standing, he pulled the blanket around his shoulders. His mind seemed muddled. "What is this place?" he said aloud, and was startled by the sound. Looking around, he saw that he was in a little clearing in some woods. Part of him seemed to remember that he had been wandering for weeks, avoiding towns and stealing food, but another part of him stood apart and simply watched. Words formed in his mind: "Stan, this is not going to be fun." The words were not from the voice he had heard when he had spoken.

Somewhere in the distance he heard voices. An old fear reasserted itself, reminding him that he was exposed in the center of the clearing. He felt for the pistol in his pants pocket and moved to the shelter between two big trees.

"Hey, Stan!" It was a familiar voice, somebody coming toward the clearing. "Hey, you wicked son of a bitch, don't shoot me."

The figure in jungle fatigues seemed familiar, as well. Stan felt weird; he recognized Andrew, and yet he couldn't move from his position. Finally, he waved and let the blanket fall from his shoulders. "Here I am, Buddy," he said.

Andrew laughed. "You're cool, Stan," he said. "Campbell and the guys are gonna find some food down at that farm. "Wanna come?"

Stan stepped out into the clearing. "I'm messed up, Man," he said, scratching his head. "Somethin's happened to me."

"What?"

"Don' know. My head's messed up." Stan picked up his coat from next to the campfire and put it on.

"This is very interesting," said a voice in his head. "These must be his friends."

Stan shook his head and pounded on the side of his skull with a fist.

"You high, Stan?" Andrew came closer, peering into Stan's face. "C'mon, let's get some food in you. You look like warmed-over death."

Two other men, that Stan knew only as traveling companions of Andrew, followed the two down the path. Stan kept trying to clear his head by shaking it vigorously from side to side.

"I'm not connecting," said the voice in his head. "But at least we're with other people. They can lead us for a while until I get connected." Stan thought he knew the voice, but it wasn't his.

In sight of a cluster of old buildings, the other three men crouched behind some bushes. "There aren't any cars, just that old pickup truck."

"Get down, Stan," said Andrew. "If you aren't cool, you stay here and we'll go in."

One of the men laughed and said, "What would you like for breakfast, Stanley? Maybe an omelet?"

"Wise ass," grumbled another. "Keep quiet. Let's go."

Stan watched the three move quickly across the open yard. After a minute, they disappeared into the house. They were gone for what seemed a long time.

The voice seemed uncertain. "They aren't going to harm anyone, are they?"

"I don't think so," whispered Stan. He continued to peer through the tall grass at the house. Startled by his own voice, he tried to understand who he was talking to.

This was a new thing. Ever since he'd left the hospital, Stan was frequently troubled by memories of chaos, of sounds and concussive pressures on his body, of going in and out of consciousness, and of white rooms. People trying to make him understand that he needed to calm down. "Be cool, Stanley," the pretty nurse kept cooing to him. "You have to heal."

She had dark brown hair, and sometimes she let him see it falling down over her shoulders instead of tucked inside that white hat. He knew that he could heal if she would just stay with him. He called her Cherry although that's not how she pronounced it.

But the stuff at night—the noise and the fear— always came back, and he had to get out of there.

They let him get dressed for meals, his old fatigues having been washed and repaired. After dinner one evening—the days were getting shorter, and it was almost dark—he simply walked out the door when nobody else was around.

He hitched rides out of town and began to wander. There was no place he wanted to go; it was just that having people around seemed to keep him confused. Being off the roads in the forest gave him a sense of safety. Maybe he could figure out how to get rid of the night stuff in his head.

Now he wasn't sure. This voice in his head was new. It seemed to know him, and yet it didn't. Some of the guys on the ward had told him that they heard voices, too, but they were off their rockers and didn't make sense when they talked.

Besides frequent hunger, Stan had felt something going on in his chest. He'd take deep breaths when it hurt, trying to overcome the pain. Sometimes it had worked.

The guys reappeared from the farmhouse, carrying plastic bags of stuff. They ran crouching to his position.

Andrew held up his bag. "Food," he said grinning. Stan followed them back into the woods.

"Anybody in there?" Stan asked them, remembering the voice and hoping nobody had been hurt in the house.

"No, they were gone. It was just our own little grocery store."

The men found another small clearing and built a fire. One held up a can of tuna. "Don't need can openers anymore," he laughed, and peeled the top from the can.

"They had lots of soup," Andrew said. "I don't think they live there very much. The fridge was empty except for beer."

⊷—⊶

Andrew had found Stan one evening the week before, huddled inside a kind of tent he had made out of shrubbery trying to keep warm.

"Man," he had said, "we got to get you some clothes, blankets and stuff. You'll freeze out here in a few weeks." He took Stan into a Salvation Army store nearby and helped him pick out some things. Inviting Stan to tag along with them, the little band explored the rural area, seldom sleeping in the same place more than once.

Andrew had slipped him the pistol one day out of sight of the others. "These guys'll treat you okay, but they'll take this from you if they see it." He grinned. "Just keep it to yourself. Never know who you'll run into."

Later, Stan had examined the pistol. It was a Glock, familiar to him, and seemed in good condition, with a full clip. In Syria, he'd handled a lot of weapons. Feeling its weight in his pocket gave him a feeling of safety.

"This is a weapon?" the voice asked him.

"Yes," he said softly, then frowned and looked around. "Where are you?" he demanded, his voice louder.

"There's been a mistake," the voice said. "You're not supposed to be here anymore."

Stan sat down suddenly on the ground. Holding his head between his hands, he thought, *I'm going nuts, just like those guys on the ward.*

"You were supposed to have died the other night," said the voice. "I was supposed to take your place."

"No, no, no!" said Stan aloud, and shook his head.

"You had a heart attack, and were supposed to die in your sleep."

Stan slumped back against a small tree.

"We aren't sure what to do now." said the voice.

"Who are you? What d'you want from me?"

"I'm here to observe. You aren't supposed to be here anymore."

"You mean I'm dead?"

The voice paused. "That's the problem. You're not."

Stan thought about that for a while. He remembered the pain and the strange feeling in his chest the other night. "You tried to kill me," he said, feeling resigned.

"No, we don't do that."

"Whyn't you go someplace else?"

"We have to wait for this to get straightened out."

"I *am* crazy," said Stan.

"I don't think so," said the voice in his head. "Just try to stay calm until we get this straightened out."

"Jesus Christ!"

"I know, it's frustrating."

Stan frowned. "So I'm stuck with you." Then he thought of the hospital. "Hey, all those guys back on the ward, saying they heard voices—that was you?"

Another long pause. "I don't think so. This is very unusual."

"You know, if Andrew and the guys heard me talking to you, they'd figure I belonged back on that ward."

"You don't have to talk out loud. I can hear you thinking." Then it added, "and when you remember things."

Stan thought for a moment. "So you know I escaped from the hospital."

"When you remember it, so do I."

"Jesus Christ!" He looked around to see if Andrew's bunch was nearby. He squeezed his head between his palms. "It's like that old Pink Floyd song, 'There's someone in my head and it ain't me!'

The thought made him grin in spite of his confusion. "Boy could I have something to talk about back on the ward!"

"Please be patient," said the voice.

Stan could hear the guys talking over on the other side of the woods, but he was curious. "Tell me," he thought in words, "Who are you, anyway? Why are you inside my head?"

"I'm here to observe. I've never had a living mind to deal with. I have to piece a human together so I can interact with others."

"You still haven't told me who you are!" Stan was getting impatient.

"I don't know how to tell you so you could understand."

"Well, shit. Would you just get out? I don't need this!"

"Yes, I understand. Actually," said the voice, sounding different somehow, "this is an interesting situation. Usually we don't have a live mind to study. Our observations usually come from communicating with other humans."

"You're some kind of alien anthropologists?"

"Well," said the voice, "that's an interesting way to put it."

Stan heard the other guys approaching. "Well," he whispered, "just shut up, will you? For now, just shut up and let me think. I can't be listening to you and listening to them at the same time!"

Although the voice remained quiet, Stan couldn't focus on what the guys were talking about. He heard them discussing the possibility of moving into the farm house while the owners were gone.

"But they're going to come back sometime!" one of them whined.

"We can rig up a trip wire on the road to let us know they're coming."

Andrew laughed. "Or an IUD."

At that, the others all laughed. Stan, barely able to get the words out through his laughter, said, "You mean, IED?"

"Oh, yeah, IED."

"You weren't in Iraq, were you?" asked Stan. All four men were still laughing.

"Thinking of something else," Andrew said, no longer laughing.

"Your girlfriend," somebody offered, setting off the laughter again.

"We could get a tree across the road," Stan said. "That would slow them down enough to let us get out of the house. And it wouldn't make them suspicious."

"Good thinking," said Andrew.

"Aw, I want to hit 'em with an IUD!" someone else said.

The four men made their way through the brush to the access road to the farmhouse. Just out of sight of the main road, they picked out a dead tree that leaned at a precarious angle over the drive. "We ought to be able to pull that down with just a rope."

Finding a rope in one of the outbuildings, they pulled the tree across the drive. "Looks like the wind did it."

Stan was enjoying the good-natured resourcefulness of the group, and forgot the voice, which remained silent.

Two

The four men settled into the old farmhouse, freely using the food they found there. They agreed on a signal that would be used in case there was a sign that the owners—or anyone else—were approaching. A large pan was hung next to the kitchen door, with a heavy spoon dangling from it, to be used as an alarm. The group was to scatter into the nearby woods but remain near enough to confirm the intrusion, and collect in a clearing to decide what to do next.

Stan, with urging from his visiting Voice, learned the names of the other two men: Campbell, who was a little older than the others and had no military experience, and Slade, who had served in Afghanistan like Andrew. Both were easy-going, having no particular ambitions other than to remain free and fed. They all enjoyed living "off the grid," as Andrew put it. Even though they stole food and such necessities as blankets and shoes, they carried no animosity toward society.

Stan thought that he would remain with the group for a while as long as it felt comfortable, but eventually would return somehow to the "real world."

He and his Voice developed a working relationship. When no one was around, they conversed mostly about how Stan related to the other men. The Voice also seemed curious about Stan's night fears.

"I've noticed that you have trouble sleeping," it said. "Your dreams are filled with anxiety and dread."

"Yeah. The doctors told me I have PTSD from my time in Syria. I thrash around in my sleep a lot."

"That's why you were in a hospital?"

"Yeah, but the meds they gave me didn't do any good, and I hated being there."

"So you 'escaped.'"

"I escaped."

"You just wanted to run around in the woods and steal your food." Voice was learning about Stan.

"I'm out here because people drive me crazy," Stan said. "I like the quiet."

"Were you always like that?"

"No," Stan laughed. "I used to be just a regular guy. I had friends and a job. You know."

"Is this condition permanent?"

"The doctors said no, but some guys get over it quicker than others."

"So, it's like a bruise in the mind."

Stan frowned. "I guess. Why?"

Voice was quiet for a few moments. Then it said, "I wonder if it can be healed more quickly. Then perhaps you could go back into your former life."

"That's what the docs were trying to do. I just couldn't deal with the process."

"When you sleep tonight, I will see what can be done."

"You mean—"

"We have techniques." It paused again.

Stan grinned. "I'm getting to know you," he said. "I can tell when you're 'just observing,' as you called it, and when you're thinking—or whatever it is you do."

That night, Stan slept better than he had in a long time. As he awakened just after dawn, he was aware of feeling different. He always slept apart from the other guys, saying that he needed to be alone so he wouldn't keep people awake with his yelling in his sleep.

"You up yet?" he whispered.

Voice answered immediately, "I don't have to close down, to sleep as you do."

"I feel, like, more relaxed or something."

"Good."

"You do something to my head?"

"We'll see. It may take a while to tell if it worked."

"What'd you do?"

"There was a kind of knot in your brain that didn't look normal. I untangled some of it."

"That my PTSD?" Stan was suddenly curious.

"Perhaps."

"Wow."

L ater, as the group scavenged a local strip mall for discarded food, even Andrew noticed a change in Stan. "Your voice is lower or something," he said quietly. "You get ahold of some weed?"

"No," answered Stan. "I just woke up kinda relaxed this morning."

As the days went on, he was aware of feeling less tense in the face of uncertainty, and found it easier to banter with the group. He began to think about the rest of the world and wondered if he could bear to be out in the open again.

One day as they strolled past a pizza restaurant, he noticed a "Drivers Needed" sign.

He dug his driver's license from his back pack and went in. The manager looked him up and down and asked a lot of questions, but didn't seem to care that he was not a clean-cut young man. "Stanley, you have to be prompt," he said, "and account for the money. You can keep your tips, but we want our share. Okay?"

"Sure."

"Just remember, you're gonna be in our car. People will judge us by how you act."

"Okay," Stanley assured him.

"You know how to work the GPS?"

"I think so. They're all different."

The manager took him out to the car and showed him how to operate the instrument. Then he looked over at him. "No alcohol, no drugs, understand?"

"Yep."

"You're on probation for a week. One bad move, and you're out. I mean, immediately!"

"Gotcha."

Stanley was impressed with his own ability to fit into the needs of the real world. He could do this. He had Andrew trim his beard, and he made sure his clothes were reasonably clean and neat for his first day on the job.

He was eager to share his new sense of himself with Voice, who had remained silent throughout the interview and the rest of the day. When he turned in that evening, he whispered, "Gotta hand it to you."

"As long as I'm stuck here with you," Voice said, "might as well make the best of it."

Stanley laughed. "Got a bum assignment, huh?"

"I don't quite understand that."

"I was making a joke. I guess you don't get humor. A lot of people are given jobs that they don't like."

About a week after the group moved into the farm house, they heard heavy equipment operating out near the road. Someone was apparently moving their barricade from the drive. They quickly gathered their belongings and fled into the woods.

Stanley took that opportunity to separate from the group and find a cheap motel not far from the pizza restaurant. When he returned the pistol to Andrew, he wished him luck. "I don't need to hide out in the woods anymore," he said.

As he earned enough money delivering pizzas, he bought more presentable clothing. He felt he was re-entering the real world.

Three

Stanley's night panics diminished. He and Voice carried on conversations while he delivered pizza. "We haven't talked about you lately," he said one day. "You're obviously not just a figment of my imagination. You fixed my head—I don't think I'm going nuts anymore, and I feel pretty good. I like working for a living again."

"I don't seem to have as much access to your memory or your emotional state as I expected," said Voice. "I can perceive your current thoughts and sensations."

"Already my boss is talking about bringing me into the restaurant. That'll mean more money, but you and I may not have as much chance to chat while I'm working."

"I understand."

"Y'know," Stanley said, "you don't make me nervous like you used to. It's like having a buddy with me wherever I go." He laughed. "And you don't borrow money from me!"

"I've detected something else going on with you recently," said Voice as Stanley drove away from a delivery. "The way you react when you are near a young woman."

Stanley laughed again. "You caught that, did you? I just looked at that woman, and I have to admit I felt something."

"Is that what you call normal?"

Stanley couldn't speak for a moment as he continued to laugh. "Boy, have you got a lot to learn!"

"I'm here to observe," Voice said.

Stanley pounded his forehead and grinned. "That was a joke, wasn't it? You do have a sense of humor!"

"You were sexually attracted to her?"

"You think?" The grin stayed on his face.

Pulling into the restaurant parking lot, Stanley locked the car and went inside. The cashier watched while he counted out the receipts from his delivery trip. "You're making good tips," she said, and looked up at him. "I'm not surprised. You make a good impression on people."

"You wouldn't know that six months ago I was in a nut ward, would you?

She looked startled. "I don't believe you!"

"PTSD," he said. "I think I'm cured."

"You were in combat?"

"Syria. Special Forces."

She smiled. "Well, I'm glad you made it back in one piece."

His face became serious. "Not everybody did."

His boss promoted him to dispatcher, and he spent his shift organizing the drivers and making sure the pizzas were delivered promptly. It was an easy job for Stanley, and he made friends with the other people working in the restaurant. He never let on that he had a voice in his head with whom he chatted when nobody else was around.

The restaurant staff turned over frequently. Cooks and wait staff tended to stay for short times then move on to other jobs.

One new hire, Kathy, a woman who, while bright enough and attractive, seemed to be unsure of herself. The boss made her a hostess, greeting customers and leading them to their tables. She smiled at everybody, and Stanley took a liking to her at once. She showed a shyness that appealed to him.

Voice, however, seemed unimpressed with her. "You would be wise to keep your distance," he told Stanley.

"Why?"

"I believe you'll be disappointed."

"She's new," Stanley protested, "she needs some support. This place gets pretty hectic sometimes, and the hostess has to deal with impatient customers."

Voice let the subject drop, but Stanley could tell that he (or "it"—he wasn't sure) didn't approve when he stood by the hostess station and chatted with Kathy.

Once, when both he and Kathy were preparing to leave at the end of the day, he suggested that they have a drink together.

"I'd like that," she said with a smile. "Where do you usually go?"

"I only know of one place—I'm pretty new in town, too."

At the Bistro on the far side of town, they found a quiet corner. It was late for the after-dinner crowd, and there was no live music that night.

"Where did you come from?" he asked her.

"I live up near Dayton," she said. "It's a good drive to work, but I'm planning to get a place closer as soon as I can."

"You haven't had much experience in restaurants, have you?"

"No. I used to live with a fellow in Dayton, but I was in an accident and spent some months in the hospital." She looked down and smiled. "He got tired of waiting."

He told her about his tour in Syria and his resulting hospitalization. "What do you really like to do?" he asked.

She showed him her shy smile. "I don't know," she said, "I guess mostly I write poetry." Laughing, she elaborated, "Can't make a living doing that."

"What did you do before?"

She looked down at her hands. "I can't remember."

When he looked quizzically at her she said, "I don't remember much before that accident."

"Wow." A surge of feeling rose in Stanley's throat. He remembered all the nights he spent in the hospital trying to forget the awful experiences he'd had in Syria.

"Is that like amnesia?" he asked.

"I guess so. I had a bad concussion."

"Do you remember your childhood, your family, ..."

"Just pieces. I've been trying to put my life together again. That's why I write poetry."

"You think there's stuff you don't want to remember?" Stanley told her that he had a lot of experiences overseas he definitely didn't want to remember.

"Careful, Stanley," Voice said in his head. "Don't go there."

Stanley frowned. He was suddenly uneasy. "I guess we ought to talk about something else."

She looked at him. "All right." Then she touched his hand. "Stanley, if it would help you to talk about it, I'd be glad to just listen."

He shook his head.

The good feeling he'd been having about the evening and about Kathy dissipated. In its place was an anxiety that he couldn't identify. After they finished their drink, he made an excuse to leave and they went out to their cars.

"See you tomorrow," he said simply.

She had a worried look on her face. "I hope I didn't say anything—"

"No," he said. "Just need to think for a while."

On the drive home, he asked Voice, "What's going on? I can talk about that stuff—some of it, anyway."

"Stanley," said Voice, "there's something you need to know."

"What?" He took a deep breath.

"It's not about you. You're doing okay. It's about her."

"What, for Christ's sake?"

"She is not really there."

"What d'you mean?"

"Remember, she said she had been in an accident? Well, she didn't survive."

It hit Stanley in the gut. He couldn't speak.

"You would not want to get involved with her. Do you understand what I'm saying?"

"You mean—"

"Kathy is not really Kathy. She's inhabited."

"Inhabited."

"I tried to contact her, but I'm too much tangled up with your mind. She couldn't hear me."

"Jesus."

"And," Voice said, "I'm hearing that the mix-up about you and me is being resolved."

"What's that mean?"

"I'll be leaving you. You're in no danger. Your heart is stronger. You'll be okay."

Stanley felt his heart beating wildly. "That's normal," said Voice. "You just had a jolt, but you'll recover. The dreams should mostly disappear, too."

Stanley was silent, trying to take in what had just happened. He drove home and lay down on his bed, his mind whirling. He thought of the weeks with Voice as a companion, almost a friend, and he thought about Kathy and what knowing her would mean to him. He couldn't fathom a relationship with her, knowing that she was not really a human being.

When he spoke to Voice, there was no answer.

He lay awake most of the night. Finally, he knew that he had to leave, leave this town and start his life over someplace else.

The End

Whale Song

One

"This is interesting," Waldo said. "A few ounces of alcohol—I'm partial to gin, myself—relaxes certain neural areas of the brain, diminishing the ordinary behavioral controls of the cerebral cortex."

I watched him grinning to himself without any self-consciousness. Waldo was clearly having fun. We'd been sitting in my living room talking, and it had been clear to me that he could be one of those *aliens* inhabiting the body of some poor human who'd had the misfortune to die just when *they* were attending to things.

He was, I thought, getting used to the complexities of the human mind. "He" remembered things the former inhabitant remembered, and I could see the contortions he had to go through to be "in" the body.

He continued, "The world does, indeed, look differently through this lens."

I guess I just grinned, for he added, "You're enjoying this, aren't you?"

I didn't say anything. I'd been here before, and I didn't have any particular feeling about *them*. I'd never met one who seemed threatening in any way. To me it was more comical than anything. *They*—if they are in any understandable way "plural"—have been having a hard time understanding human beings. It's like a retriever struggling to understand its first "fetch!"

command. Waldo and I'd had some long conversations that day, and our relationship was casual and friendly.

"You've been developing this chemical compound over centuries," he said, "What a grand time it is, watching the subtle differences in effects of various combinations of the distillation process. I've tried several psychogenic compounds, and alcohol seems the most entertaining."

"It works for me," I said, sipping the vodka martini I'd poured for myself. Waldo, when invited, had turned up his nose at first, but he drank one down. I was curious what it would do for him.

He had sort of invited himself to my place after we met in the bar down on State Street that afternoon. The Red Fox was crowded, and we couldn't hear each other very well, so I suggested that it was quieter at my place.

It seems that his previous incarnation, if that's the right term, was a college professor of marine biology who had died from a heart attack in front of his class. Waldo woke up in the E.R. and insisted upon checking himself out before the next of kin were even notified.

"You know, you humans have pretty much taken over this planet," he said. "With your communication media, nothing can get past you." He downed a second martini like it was water. "Still, you have no idea what other creatures do with their environment."

"Gimme a forinstance," I said, aware that I was slurring my words.

"Do you know that the blue whale's brain could contain everything your species has ever thought?"

"Well," I said, "why hasn't it?"

He looked at me in a funny way, like he couldn't understand where I was coming from. "How do you know it hasn't?"

"They just go swimming around out there in the ocean. What else do they do?"

Waldo sighed. "Jesus," he said, and kinda closed down.

A little while later, he looked up at me and said, "What do you know about your planet?"

"I don't know much, but I've seen a lot of it with Google Earth. You can almost see individual people on the beaches at Del Ray. What can a whale see? What's he know about, say, Ann Arbor?"

"You humans think that because you can kill every other creature on the planet that you're 'the top of the food chain,' as you claim."

I shrugged.

He squinted slightly. "What you call wisdom is just an accumulation of information by your species, disseminated in various languages over time, about how stuff works."

It was amusing for me, even as muzzy as I was feeling, to watch him struggle. Obviously, the human part of him was having a ball, but the alien part was in over his head. "You sound like a pontificating professor emeritus," I said. "Wisdom isn't just information."

He grinned. "I know more than I can tell."

"How is that working for you?" I asked, draining the last three drops from my beautiful little cone-shaped glass and peering at him through its side.

"Tacit knowledge. A man named Michael Polanyi explained it."

I shook my head and grinned back. "You learned that from me, three hours ago."

Waldo looked confused at first, then smiled. "I did, indeed, didn't I?"

"Good thing whales don't drink alcohol," I said. "They could do some real damage, with all that brain power."

He leaned back in his chair and looked at the ceiling. "I wonder," he finally said, "how much of a whale's knowledge is tacit knowledge."

"Maybe all of it?"

Something hit me. "I would have thought," I said, "that you or your kind would have inhabited whales by now. How do you know they have so much knowledge?"

He sighed. "I believe that was tried, about five hundred years ago."

"What do you mean?"

"It seems that their brains are so much more complicated than those of humans. Impervious, almost, to *inhabiting*."

"You mean we aren't much of a challenge."

He sat up. Picking up his glass, he signaled "more."

I wasn't sure, by that point, whether "more" would be a good idea. He was about two hundred pounds, close to my weight, but he was—or had been—younger and with a much better build. Some guys get unpredictable when they've had too much booze. Sober, Waldo was a pussycat. Never hurt a fly, I think.

"Alcohol can be toxic in too high a concentration," I said, trying to sound erudite.

He put his glass down.

"Sorry, Waldo," I said. "Maybe that's where human experience just might be significant, even to you."

His eyes were slightly bloodshot. I had to laugh. "You look like a boss I once had," I said, "who used to invite his customers out for lunch, you know, to get in their good graces."

Waldo smiled. "I understand."

"Well, my boss used to drink a lot at those lunches. I guess the customers did, too, but he would get so drunk we'd have to lead him out to the car."

He frowned, and began to stand up. "Whoa!" His arms went out as if to steady himself.

I laughed. "Where did you hear that word?"

"I don't know. It just came out."

"More of that tacit knowledge," I said. "Anyway, I guess you're feeling the booze."

"Quite unsteady." He sat back down.

I went into the kitchen and returned with a box of Triscuits. "Eating something might help," I said, dumping a few of the crackers into the decorative bowl on the coffee table.

"So tell me more about whales," I said.

"The adult sperm whale brain is four hundred eighty-eight cubic inches. Our brain," and he pointed to his own head, "is about seventy-nine cubic inches. It took a lot of brain power to transform the whale from a mammal something like a small hippopotamus into a totally aquatic mammal." He stopped and thought for a moment. "but that still doesn't account for the present size of the whale's brain. Neuroanatomical evidence suggests that the large whale brain supports a complex intelligence that is driven by the socially complex and highly communicative lifestyle of these predators."

Waldo leaned back and smiled at me.

"Wow," I said. "I have to hand it to you. You've got a lot of Wikipedia stored in your seventy-nine cubic inches. But I can't imagine why they need all that power for just swimming around in the ocean."

He looked down. "Yes," he said slowly, "that's why I'm here talking with you and not out there in the Pacific Ocean communicating with another whale up in the Aleutian Islands."

"You took the easier class."

Waldo frowned. "That's putting it rather strongly, isn't it?"

My face felt hot. "Sorry," I said, "My social skills are diminished by martinis."

He studied his empty martini glass. "Actually, humans were the obvious choice to study at this moment in time."

"Why is that?" I thought, *you mean point in time— moment already means time.*

Looking directly at me, he said, "Because you are indeed at the top of the food chain here, but you are also capable of destroying all life on the planet. Perhaps that could be diverted somehow."

"You want to save us from ourselves?" I was thinking about pouring some more vodka.

"Save not only you," he said. "Those whales, for example."

I nibbled on a Triscuit. "Whales shall inherit the earth? I thought that was to be the roaches."

Waldo looked at me—shocked or merely puzzled, I couldn't tell.

"Sorry," I said. "I was being funny."

"I once knew a fox terrier who was funnier."

We both laughed at that.

"So," I began, "I've met a few 'people' like you, but I've never found out just why you're doing what you're doing."

"I'm here to learn," he said with a slight smile.

I sighed and mixed myself another martini. Holding the bottle of vermouth up, I looked at him questioningly.

He nodded. I mixed another one.

"You just said you wanted to save the planet. You've got an objective, then, right?"

He shrugged and sipped at his drink.

"I'd better fix us something more substantial than whole-wheat crackers." I got up and headed for the kitchen. Over my shoulder, I said, "Do you eat meat, or are you a vegetarian?"

When he didn't respond, I stopped and looked back at him. He had sloshed a bit of his martini on his shirt front.

"What?" I asked.

"I'll never get used to you humans."

"I'll take that as a 'Yes, you're a vegetarian.'" I went to the refrigerator and dug out a mac-and-cheese casserole left over from two days ago. Loading it into the microwave, I returned to the living room, where Waldo had finished his martini.

"It's not vegan," I said. "It's got cheese in it."

He slumped back and closed his eyes. "I know it's not," he said, "but it feels as though the room is spinning." He smiled at the mixed meanings.

I dashed for the hall closet and brought back a bucket. "Just in case you feel like you're going to vomit," I said.

I shouldn't have given him that last martini.

We sat for a few minutes until the microwave dinged.

The food helped both of us. I watched him closely as we ate. As I said, he looked to be younger than I (which isn't saying much), and in pretty good shape for somebody who had "survived" a heart attack.

"I'm curious," I said, "how you happened to get into this particular person."

Waldo was curiously nonchalant in explaining. "He was clearly gone, but not damaged beyond repair. No close relatives." Like that explained everything.

He paused, then went on. "Afterward, I took a leave of absence from my academic post 'to recuperate', and they generously allowed me to disappear for a while. Maybe after I put his recent life back together in my mind, I will return to teaching. If I don't, I have the resources to do other things."

"You said you're here to learn. Sounds to me like you have more agenda than that. You mentioned saving the earth from us, or something like that."

He smiled. "Wouldn't you? If you saw some creature about to cause a major catastrophe and you might be able to prevent it, wouldn't you?"

"I don't know," I said. "There's also something to be said for allowing the creature to figure out for himself or herself what needs to be done, provided I've already satisfied myself that they have the wisdom to recover from the situation."

His eyebrow went up. "You think humans have the necessary wisdom?"

"I think from what you said earlier that you don't—maybe just don't yet—understand what 'wisdom' really is." I was feeling on thin ice. This man, or creature, or being—whatever it was—could run circles around me in knowledge and intelligence. But something was lacking.

Waldo just looked at me.

"We know," I said, "collectively we know what needs to be done to prevent catastrophic destruction to ourselves and the earth."

He looked skeptical.

I laughed. "I know, I know. We don't even know what's in a whale's mind. Maybe we have a lot to learn, but there's enough of us who know already how to solve the biggest problems that threaten us and the rest of life on Earth."

He continued to eat the mac and cheese. But I could tell that he was thinking. Maybe *he* or *they* really are here to learn.

I was warming up. "There's an old term—'faith'—that's used to justify various religious assumptions. It means trusting something, some philosophy, some generalized notion that has very large implications. I have faith that we humans are able to resolve most of the problems we have encountered or even caused ourselves. I'm willing to go with that faith rather than hope that some outside force—even yours—will come in to save us, because that would leave us in a place of—"

"Subservience?"

I was surprised by his word. He was hearing me. Frankly, I was embarrassed, because I wasn't all that confident that I knew what I was talking about. But he heard me. I just nodded.

"Thank you," he said. "I've learned something."

We sat for a long while without talking. I felt as though I should continue, but something told me that I should stop there. What else could I say that would make how I felt more clear to him? Or to me?

Finally, he scraped the last of the food from his plate and looked up at me. "I need to process," he mumbled.

He stood up carefully. Smiling, he said, "I seem to have recovered my balance."

We shook hands as he went out the door. I poured another drink and sat and thought. That he and I might never see each other again seemed almost pre-ordained. You know, "ships that pass in the night" kind of thing. I was only slightly curious about him, where he was going, how he had come about.

I didn't touch my drink. Instead, I pulled out my laptop and started a new document. There was something I needed to write, but my mind was still foggy. At least I needed, right then while Waldo was fresh in my mind, to begin something.

I typed: *It's Up to Us.*

Then I leaned back on the sofa and thought about what I had said to Waldo, that I had faith in humanity, despite the current sorry state of the world. *Of course* we don't need a messiah to save us from ourselves. If we can't do it by ourselves, we don't deserve to continue.

Perhaps whales, with their tremendous brains, know things we don't yet know. Still, they don't have history and books that can survive the inevitable passing of individuals; maybe they need all that brain power to store the wisdom that we keep in our libraries and database servers.

With our opposable thumbs, we have created vast civilizations—literally extensions of the seventy-nine-cubic inches of storage each of us carries around in our skulls, not only extending the reach of our individual minds but collecting everything that our über-compatriots have generated over the years. The wisdom that one person collects in a brief lifetime compounds exponentially in contact with that of other persons.

A whale may not feel the need to know that she has evolved from some land mammal for evolutionary reasons millions of whale lifetimes ago. Perhaps what she can communicate with others of her kind across thousands of miles of water is enough. With our minuscule brains we've figured out how to do that, too. And much more.

I thought of an essay I read in the Times that morning, "We Are Not Born Human," By Bernard-Henri Lévy, where he said:

"Humanity is not a form of being; it is not a steady state, delivered once and for all, but a process."

I went back to the Times for more, and happened on another piece, by Ai Weiwei, a Chinese expatriate, on the same subject:

"There is no such thing as a human being in the abstract. Only when we see people as embedded in their experiences—their own social positions, their educations and memories, in

pursuit of their own ideals—can the question "What is a human being?" fully make sense.

"Simply to avoid the question is a terrible mistake. We must ask it, and we must do so repeatedly. The debates and judgments that led to human wisdom in the past were responses, each in its time, to essentially the same question, asked in the political and social context of that time, and it is relevant at every social level: individual, community, family and nation. Many of the political and cultural disagreements that we see in the world today arise from a reluctance to face this key question squarely, and to arrive at clear definitions with regard to it."

"Waldo should read that," I said out loud. I didn't know how I could put any of that into my own words. (Do whales have anything like words, those magical little bits of language that combine so readily with each other to allow one to say just about anything about anything?) Words, like the little blooms in my lover's flower garden, come and go, but remind me, over and over, about what's important.

I must have dozed off. The laptop screen had gone dark, asleep like me but, like me, not lost. I hunched over the keyboard and pressed a key...

Two

For the next week I found myself thinking about Waldo. He had never said just what *they* were doing, spying on humans from inside us. I felt that he had more that he could tell me. But I had no idea how to pursue my questions with him. It was as though we'd just bumped into each other and had not arranged to meet again.

Gradually, I lost interest and occupied myself with my usual activities: working out at the gym, watching weird things on Netflix, trying to write on my current novel.

I was surprised, then, to run into him at a luncheon restaurant up on Plymouth Road that I almost never patronize. He simply nodded when our eyes met, and I took my coffee cup over and sat down at his table.

I laughed. "I haven't been in this place in years," I said. "And here you are."

Waldo smiled.

I sipped my coffee. "I have been thinking about you, though."

His eyes narrowed in a slight smile. "Whales."

Something stirred inside me. "How'd you know?"

He shrugged. "Just guessed. What did you want to ask me?"

"You said a whale's brain was big enough to hold all of the knowledge of all human beings."

"No, not exactly." He pursed his lips, a gesture I remembered seeing the last time we were together, and I waited for his "professor" side to light up.

"Actually, the sperm whale's brain is pretty big. I might have used that to make a point. The real point, of course, is that some whales—the oceanic dolphins—have an EQ second only to humans."

I guess I frowned, for he laughed. "EQ is just the ratio between brain size and body size."

"So that's not the same as IQ."

"No."

"Dolphins might be almost as smart as us?"

"Dolphins, killer whales, spinner, bottlenose…"

"So why haven't you 'inhabited' some dolphins?"

He leaned back and sighed. "I'm not sure I can put this so you can understand it."

Draining my cup, I sat back and folded my arms. "Try me."

"At this moment," he said, "This is me. I'm Waldo. I also have access to things beyond me. In some ways I am more than Waldo. Since long before Waldo, that 'something more' has observed the humans on this planet, as well as all the other life forms here."

He picked up a piece of toast and chewed the corner, then sipped from his coffee. "You're aware, I'm sure, that humanity as you know it is a late comer to Earth. Let's say only in the last ten thousand years, maybe a bit more, have you been *civilized*."

I nodded, and lifted my empty cup so the waiter could see it.

"Whales evolved," he said, "as we now know them maybe fifty *million* years ago, from mammals that lived on land to fully aquatic animals. They've developed over the millennia—a long time before *homo sapiens* arrived. Most of them have had social lives, with complex systems of communication, for a very long time. You see?" He waited for me to nod.

"In the time frames of whales, human life is just a blip in history."

"Of course," I said, "I understand that."

"But do you *appreciate* it?" His eyes burned into mine.

That made me uncomfortable. He was obviously thinking on a different plane, and I wasn't sure I could follow him. "Yes," I said, "it's humbling. I'm aware that we tend to be kinda arrogant, assuming that we're 'in charge' of everything."

He kept his eyes on mine as he ate the toast.

I went on. "You're—at least you were—a marine biologist, so you know that we don't know what goes on in a whale's mind. I don't even know," and I looked across the aisle at a pretty young woman engrossed in conversation with some guy, "what's in that woman's head. There's *no way* I could know that—even if she told me."

Waldo smiled. "If you were this close to a bottle nosed dolphin," he said, "you might be even more interested in what she was thinking."

I frowned. "Yes, of course. That woman is not the least bit interested in me, but a dolphin that close could be dangerous to me."

"Nonsense."

"But if I'm in the water and there's a wild animal right there near me—could be a shark, or could be a dolphin, what difference would it make?"

"Ever hear of a dolphin attacking a human?"

I thought for a moment. "Not that I can think of. But don't they eat fish and clams and things like that? I wouldn't be seen as dinner."

"You've just answered your own question—in a way. Dolphins and their close relatives, killer whales, are predators. They eat other animals. Even sharks. But they don't attack humans in the water. There have been only a few incidents in which a human being has been injured by a dolphin or killer whale, and those have been in closed places, marine zoos and the like. I suspect that those were personal situations."

"I didn't know that." I tried to remember if I'd ever heard of a killer whale attacking a person.

"Why do you think that is?" He smiled at me.

"I don't know."

Waldo dabbed at his mouth with his napkin. "Why not ask one?"

I laughed. "How would I do that?"

"A very good question."

I didn't know where to go from there. Waldo hadn't answered my main question: why are we being studied by *them,* and why haven't *they* studied dolphins or killer whales—if those creatures are almost as smart as we are?

He anticipated my question. "Whales have been around for a very long time, but they have never shown any indication that they could blow up the world." He was smiling as he said it.

"So you're studying us so you can maybe steer us away from blowing up the world."

He chuckled.

"Wait!" I said. Something had just hit me. "Are you—?"

He leaned back and folded his arms, and it reminded me of how I had challenged him when we had begun this conversation. I half-expected him to say, "Try me."

"Try me." He almost sounded like me.

I had to laugh. "You *do* inhabit their minds!"

Even as I laughed and watched him chuckle, my mind was whirling.

I pictured one of those Sea World places, with a bottle-nosed dolphin coming up out of the water to "kiss" a little girl standing beside it, and an attendant tossing a small fish to the animal to reward it. The audience is applauding.

Then I remembered being on a small ship in Alaska, looking down at the bow wake we were making and seeing maybe a dozen dolphins swimming ahead of us— *playing with us.*

And the vague memory of reading about a dolphin saving the life of a boy who had been injured in the water, by herding him toward shore.

"I'm here to observe," Waldo said quietly, and he picked up his check and walked out.

Three

What is it like to be a human?

I kept thinking about Waldo. He was obviously something other than human— perhaps wearing the body of a human. In my cogitating, I used the term "alien," but I wasn't sure that term fit Waldo.

I remembered a question that I came across in my reading about consciousness: "What is it like to be a bat?" It was a philosophical-psychological question addressing the idea that "an organism has conscious mental states, if and only if there is something that it is like to be that organism—something it is like for the organism to be itself."

A weird idea, I thought. But the whole thing seemed weird; *something* inside Waldo looking out at the world, at *me,* seeing like I see, at least I think like I see. A robot endowed with artificial intelligence might move and respond to stimuli according to sophisticated internal programming, but could it be thought of as *conscious?*

I couldn't imagine what it is like to be a bat—or a whale—but I thought I should be able to get a handle on the more immediate question: What is it like to be a human?

I had those two conversations with *something* that was at least *like* a human. We talked about human things, human concerns. I sensed as we talked that Waldo had feelings similar to my own about a lot of things. He seemed to understand what I was trying to say, and to guide my thoughts. Sometimes he seemed to know what I was thinking even before I said it. *What is it like to be Waldo?*

He talked a lot about whales and dolphins. He made me admit that whales are pretty special creatures. Did that mean that he was speaking *as a whale?* Or something that knows what it's like to be a whale?

I'd heard that "aliens" like Waldo mean us no harm—indeed, they keep repeating a mantra: "I'm here to observe." What if, I wondered, Waldo and others like him (if there is a *they),* what if that consciousness is the consciousness of, say, a dolphin?

I've read that humans can be identified as the "tool users" but also that some other animals—even some birds—use tools. Opposable thumbs, likewise, do not necessarily mean human.

Nor does consciousness, in its fundamental sense.

Killer whales—orcas—seem to have some kind of consciousness. We don't know much more than that.

Short of that "much more", however, includes the fact that they do not see human beings as "dinner" or "enemy." In fact, they appear quite docile around humans who might be near them in the water. So, they *definitely know* what a human is.

Even dogs, whom we have adopted in vast numbers into our households, cannot be trusted that much. *Do dolphins know what it's like to be a human?*

Nick Pyenson, curator of fossil marine mammals at the Smithsonian Institution's National Museum of Natural History, in his book *Spying on Whales,* writes about them:

"Their size, power and intelligence in the water are astonishing because they're unparalleled, yet whales are benign and pose no threat to our lives. *They are almost a human dream of alien life: approachable, sophisticated, and inscrutable."*

He says that one coarse way to tell about the awareness of an animal is to have them look in a mirror. Only a few species other than ours can recognize themselves; among them are dolphins and—maybe—orcas.

I told Waldo that I thought he had an agenda, other than just to observe. He admitted that there could be a good reason to study humans, if nothing other than to try to steer us from our path to self-destruction.

"Save not only you," he had said. "Those whales, for example."

I didn't know when or if I would get another chance to talk with Waldo. Our two conversations seemed to have happened by coincidence. Or perhaps not.

I felt only that I'd been given a gift. The gift of a question. Maybe that's as good a gift as one can get.

I thought of what I had typed in my vodka-fogged state the first night of our talking, on an otherwise blank page:

It's Up to Us.

The End

39594426R00121

Made in the USA
Middletown, DE
22 March 2019